YORK NOTES

CW00348277

PRIDE AND PREJUDICE

JANE AUSTEN

WORKBOOK BY JULIA JONES

PEARSON

YORK PRESS

YORK PRESS
322 Old Brompton Road, London SW5 9JH

PEARSON EDUCATION LIMITED
Edinburgh Gate, Harlow,
Essex CM20 2JE, United Kingdom
Associated companies, branches and representatives throughout the world

First published 2016

10 9 8 7 6 5 4 3 2 1

ISBN 978–1–2921–3812–1

Illustrations by Iris Compiet; and Alan Batley (page 61 only)

Phototypeset by Swales and Willis Ltd
Printed in Slovakia

Photo credits: titov dmitriy/Shutterstock for page 11 / dwori/Shutterstock for page 21 / Svetlana Levachova/Shutterstock for page 23 / cynoclub/Shutterstock for page 29 / rolleiflextlr/Thinkstock for page 59 / david muscroft/Shutterstock for page 60

CONTENTS

PART FOUR:
THEMES, CONTEXTS AND SETTINGS

PART FIVE:
FORM, STRUCTURE AND LANGUAGE

PART SIX:
PROGRESS BOOSTER

PART ONE: Getting Started

Preparing for assessment

HOW WILL I BE ASSESSED ON MY WORK ON *PRIDE AND PREJUDICE*?

All exam boards are different, but whichever course you are following, your work will be examined through these three Assessment Objectives:

Assessment Objectives	Wording	Worth thinking about ...
AO1	Read, understand and respond to texts. Students should be able to: • maintain a critical style and develop an informed personal response • use textual references, including quotations, to support and illustrate interpretations.	• How well do I know what happens, what people say, do, etc.? • What do *I* think about the key ideas in the novel? • How can I support my viewpoint in a really convincing way? • What are the best quotations to use and when should I use them?
AO2	Analyse the language, form and structure used by a writer to create meanings and effects, using relevant subject terminology where appropriate.	• What specific things does the writer 'do'? What choices has Austen made? (Why this particular word, phrase or paragraph here? Why does this event happen at this point?) • What effects do these choices create? Suspense? Ironic laughter? Reflective mood?
AO3	Show understanding of the relationships between texts and the contexts in which they were written.	• What can I learn about society from the book? (What does it tell me about wealth and inheritance in Austen's day, for example?) • What was society like in Austen's time? Can I see it reflected in the text?

If you are studying OCR then you will also have a small number of marks allocated to AO4:

AO4	Use a range of vocabulary and sentence structures for clarity, purpose and effect, with accurate spelling and punctuation.	• How accurately and clearly do I write? • Are there small errors of grammar, spelling and punctuation I can get rid of?

Look out for the Assessment Objective labels throughout your York Notes Workbook – these will help to focus your study and revision!

The text used in this Workbook is the Heinemann New Windmill Classics edition, 1994.

How to use your York Notes Workbook

There are lots of ways your Workbook can support your study and revision of *Pride and Prejudice*. There is no 'right' way – choose the one that suits your learning style best.

1) Alongside the York Notes Study Guide and the text	2) As a 'stand-alone' revision programme	3) As a form of mock-exam
Do you have the York Notes Study Guide for *Pride and Prejudice*? The contents of your Workbook are designed to match the sections in the Study Guide, so with the novel to hand you could: • read the relevant section(s) of the Study Guide and any part of the novel referred to • complete the tasks in the same section in your Workbook.	Think you know *Pride and Prejudice* well? Why not work through the Workbook systematically, either as you finish chapters, or as you study or revise certain aspects in class or at home. You could make a revision diary and allocate particular sections of the Workbook to a day or week.	Prefer to do all your revision in one go? You could put aside a day or two and work through the Workbook, page by page. Once you have finished, check all your answers in one go! This will be quite a challenge, but it may be the approach you prefer.

HOW WILL THE WORKBOOK HELP YOU TEST AND CHECK YOUR KNOWLEDGE AND SKILLS?

Parts Two to **Five** offer a range of tasks and activities:

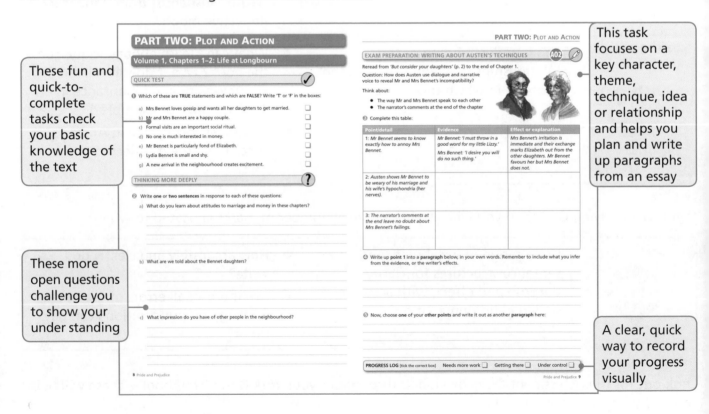

These fun and quick-to-complete tasks check your basic knowledge of the text

These more open questions challenge you to show your under standing

This task focuses on a key character, theme, technique, idea or relationship and helps you plan and write up paragraphs from an essay

A clear, quick way to record your progress visually

Each Part ends with a **Practice task** to extend your revision:

An exam-style task for you to practise a full essay

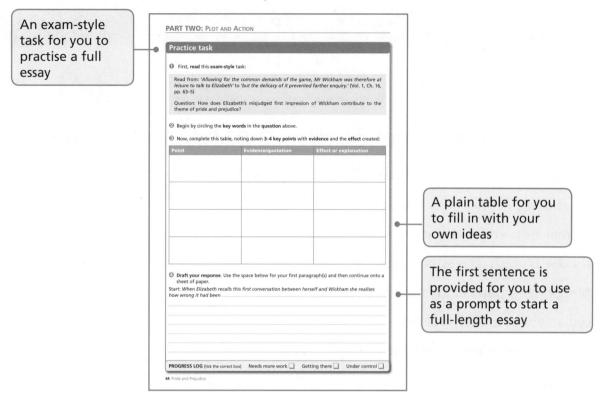

A plain table for you to fill in with your own ideas

The first sentence is provided for you to use as a prompt to start a full-length essay

Part Six: Progress Booster helps you test your own key writing skills:

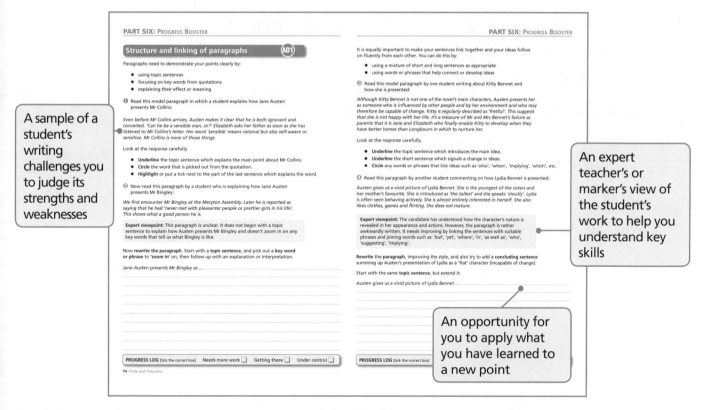

A sample of a student's writing challenges you to judge its strengths and weaknesses

An expert teacher's or marker's view of the student's work to help you understand key skills

An opportunity for you to apply what you have learned to a new point

Don't forget – these are just some examples of the Workbook contents. Inside there is much, much more to help you revise. For example:

- lots of samples of students' own work at different levels
- help with writing skills
- advice and tasks on writing about context
- a full answer key so you can check your answers
- a full-length practice exam task with guidance on what to focus on.

PART TWO: PLOT AND ACTION

Volume 1, Chapters 1–2: Life at Longbourn

QUICK TEST ✓

❶ Which of these are **TRUE** statements and which are **FALSE**? Write 'T' or 'F' in the boxes:

   a) Mrs Bennet loves gossip and wants all her daughters to get married. ☐

   b) Mr and Mrs Bennet are a happy couple. ☐

   c) Formal visits are an important social ritual. ☐

   d) No one is much interested in money. ☐

   e) Mr Bennet is particularly fond of Elizabeth. ☐

   f) Lydia Bennet is small and shy. ☐

   g) A new arrival in the neighbourhood creates excitement. ☐

THINKING MORE DEEPLY ?

❷ Write **one** or **two sentences** in response to each of these questions:

   a) What do you learn about attitudes to marriage and money in these chapters?

    ....

    ....

    ....

    ....

    ....

   b) What are we told about the Bennet daughters?

    ....

    ....

    ....

    ....

    ....

   c) What impression do you have of other people in the neighbourhood?

    ....

    ....

    ....

    ....

    ....

EXAM PREPARATION: WRITING ABOUT AUSTEN'S TECHNIQUES

Reread from *'But consider your daughters'* (p. 2) to the end of Chapter 1.

Question: How does Austen use dialogue and narrative voice to reveal Mr and Mrs Bennet's incompatibility?

Think about:

- The way Mr and Mrs Bennet speak to each other
- The narrator's comments at the end of the chapter

❸ Complete this table:

Point/detail	Evidence	Effect or explanation
1: *Mr Bennet seems to know exactly how to annoy Mrs Bennet.*	Mr Bennet: 'I must throw in a good word for my little Lizzy.' Mrs Bennet: 'I desire you will do no such thing.'	Mrs Bennet's irritation is immediate and their exchange marks Elizabeth out from the other daughters. Mr Bennet favours her but Mrs Bennet does not.
2: *Austen shows Mr Bennet to be weary of his marriage and his wife's hypochondria (her nerves).*		
3: *The narrator's comments at the end leave no doubt about Mrs Bennet's failings.*		

❹ Write up **point 1** into a **paragraph** below, in your own words. Remember to include what you infer from the evidence, or the writer's effects.

....

....

....

....

....

❺ Now, choose **one** of your **other points** and write it out as another **paragraph** here:

....

....

....

....

....

PROGRESS LOG [tick the correct box]   Needs more work ☐   Getting there ☐   Under control ☐

Volume 1, Chapters 3–6: Impressions and reactions

❶ Choose the correct answer to **finish the statement** and tick the box:

a) People are initially impressed by Mr Darcy because of his:

lively conversation ☐   good manners ☐   wealth ☐

b) Elizabeth Bennet overhears Mr Darcy describe her as:

well dressed ☐   tolerable ☐   friendly ☐

c) Bingley and Darcy's friendship is based on:

Bingley's admiration for Darcy's judgement ☐   Darcy's reliance on Bingley's cleverness ☐
Darcy's admiration for Bingley's sisters ☐

d) Charlotte Lucas thinks Jane Bennet should:

hide her feelings ☐   show her feelings ☐   not get married ☐

e) Mr Darcy begins to change his mind about Elizabeth because of her:

playfulness ☐   performance at the piano ☐   calm manners ☐

THINKING MORE DEEPLY ?

❷ Write **one** or **two sentences** in response to each of these questions:

a) What do we learn about Jane and Bingley's feelings for each other?

....

....

....

....

b) What does the narrator tell us about the Bingley sisters?

....

....

....

....

c) Do all the characters agree that pride is a bad quality? Give two contrasting views on pride from these chapters.

....

....

....

....

EXAM PREPARATION: WRITING ABOUT ATTITUDES TO MARRIAGE

Reread Chapter 6 from *'"It may perhaps be pleasant," replied Charlotte'* to *'"you would never act in this way yourself"'* (pp. 16–17).

Question: How does Austen express different female approaches to marriage?

Think about:

- The differences between Charlotte's and Elizabeth's attitudes
- The language of the scene

❸ Complete this table:

Point/detail	Evidence	Effect or explanation
1: *Charlotte thinks Jane should make every effort to get Bingley to propose.*	*'She may lose the opportunity of fixing him'.*	*Charlotte's language suggests she has a strategic approach to finding a husband.*
2: *Elizabeth says that Jane needs to be sure of her feelings and needs time to get to know Bingley.*		
3: *Austen shows that Elizabeth is unaware of the extent of the difference between herself and Charlotte.*		

❹ Write up **point 1** into a **paragraph** below, in your own words. Remember to include what you infer from the evidence, or the writer's effects:

....

....

....

....

....

❺ Now, choose **one** of your **other points** and write it out as another **paragraph** here:

....

....

....

....

....

....

PROGRESS LOG [tick the correct box]   Needs more work ☐   Getting there ☐   Under control ☐

Volume 1, Chapters 7–8: Country life in winter

QUICK TEST

❶ Complete this **gap-fill** paragraph, adding the **correct or suitable** information:

Winter in the countryside could be very dull for unmarried women of the higher social ...., who were not expected to work. Lydia and Kitty Bennet's lives are changed by the arrival of a Militia .... in the nearby town of .... where their aunt and uncle live. They walk there every day to gossip about the .... The Bingley sisters are also bored and invite Jane to .... with them. Mrs Bennet schemes for Jane to be caught in the rain so that she will have to stay for the .... Jane falls ill and Elizabeth walks across .... to be with her. The Bingley sisters are shocked by Elizabeth's ....

THINKING MORE DEEPLY ?

❷ Write **one** or **two sentences** in response to each of these questions:

a) What do Mr and Mrs Bennet think about Kitty and Lydia's visits to Meryton?

....

....

....

....

b) How does Mrs Bennet try to make sure that Jane will be asked to stay at Netherfield?

....

....

....

....

c) What accomplishments should a young lady have – in the opinion of Miss Bingley and Mr Darcy?

....

....

....

....

EXAM PREPARATION: WRITING ABOUT DIFFERENT POINTS OF VIEW

Reread Chapter 7 from '"*I admire the activity of your benevolence,*" *observed Mary*' to '*was thinking only of his breakfast*' (pp. 25–6).

Question: How is Elizabeth's three-mile walk presented and how do different characters react to it?

Think about:

- The different characters and their individual points of view
- The language Austen chooses

❸ Complete this table:

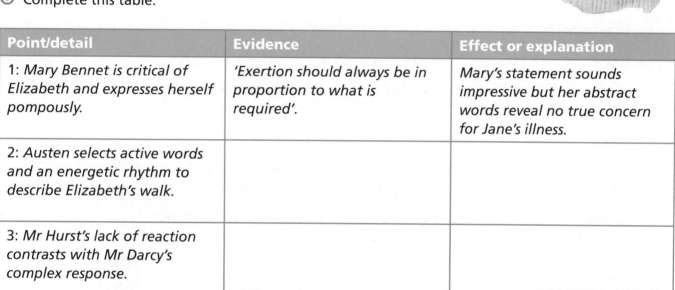

Point/detail	Evidence	Effect or explanation
1: *Mary Bennet is critical of Elizabeth and expresses herself pompously.*	'*Exertion should always be in proportion to what is required*'.	*Mary's statement sounds impressive but her abstract words reveal no true concern for Jane's illness.*
2: *Austen selects active words and an energetic rhythm to describe Elizabeth's walk.*		
3: *Mr Hurst's lack of reaction contrasts with Mr Darcy's complex response.*		

❹ Write up **point 1** into a **paragraph** below, in your own words. Remember to include what you infer from the evidence, or the writer's effects:

....
....
....
....
....

❺ Now, choose **one** of your **other points** and write it out as another **paragraph** here:

....
....
....
....
....

PROGRESS LOG [tick the correct box]   Needs more work ☐   Getting there ☐   Under control ☐

Volume 1, Chapters 9–12: Relationships at Netherfield

QUICK TEST

❶ From the list of names, identify which character (or characters) the speaker is **referring to**. Write the name (or names) next to each quotation.

Jane	Elizabeth	Mr Bingley	Miss Bingley	Mrs Hurst
	Mr Darcy	Miss Darcy	Charlotte Lucas	

a) Mrs Bennet: 'I fancy <u>she</u> was wanted about the mince pies. For my part, Mr Bingley, I always keep servants that can do their own work.' (p. 35) ....

b) Elizabeth: '<u>Your</u> defect is a propensity to hate every body.' (p. 47) ....

c) Darcy: 'And <u>yours</u> […] is wilfully to misunderstand them.' (p. 47) ....

d) Mrs Bennet: '<u>She</u> has, without exception, the sweetest temper I ever met with.' (p. 33) ....

e) Caroline Bingley: '<u>He</u> leaves out half his words, and blots the rest.' (p. 38) ....

f) Narrator: '<u>They</u> could describe an entertainment with accuracy, relate an anecdote with humour, and laugh at their acquaintance with spirit.' (p. 43) ....

g) Caroline Bingley: 'Pray let <u>her</u> know that I am quite in raptures with her beautiful little design for a table.' (p. 38) ....

THINKING MORE DEEPLY

❷ Write **one** or **two sentences** in response to each of these questions:

a) How does Mrs Bennet reveal the limitations of her world?

....

....

....

....

b) How does Caroline Bingley try to ingratiate herself with Mr Darcy?

....

....

....

....

c) How do Mr and Mrs Bennet welcome their older daughters home?

....

....

....

....

EXAM PREPARATION: WRITING ABOUT FORESHADOWING EVENTS

Reread from '"Nay," cried Bingley, "this is too much"' to 'Mr Darcy smiled; but Elizabeth thought she could perceive that he was rather offended; and therefore checked her laugh.' (pp. 39–41)

Question: What do we learn about Bingley's character and what is its significance?

Think about:

- What is being said about Bingley's decision-making
- How it will affect the plot

❸ Complete this table:

Point/detail	Evidence	Effect or explanation
1: *Bingley's overhasty decisions and his deference to Darcy are discussed at length.*	*Elizabeth: 'To yield readily – easily – to the persuasion of a friend is no merit with you.'*	*This is ironic. Elizabeth thinks she is defending Bingley's kind nature when in fact his weakness of character will hurt Jane.*
2: *Bingley leaving Netherfield is mentioned as a specific possibility.*		
3: *Austen shows Elizabeth trying to defend Bingley then realising that Darcy's feelings have been hurt.*		

❹ Write up **point 1** into a **paragraph** below, in your own words. Remember to include what you infer from the evidence, or the writer's effects:

....
....
....
....
....

❺ Now, choose **one** of your **other points** and write it out as another **paragraph** here:

....
....
....
....
....
....

PROGRESS LOG [tick the correct box]   Needs more work ☐   Getting there ☐   Under control ☐

Volume 1, Chapters 13–17: Mr Collins and Mr Wickham

QUICK TEST ✔

❶ Which of these are **TRUE** statements and which are **FALSE**? Write 'T' or 'F' in the boxes:

a) Mr Bennet gives his wife as much advance warning as possible of the guest who will be arriving at Longbourn. ☐

b) Mr Collins writes a short, clear, affectionate letter. ☐

c) Mr Collins is keen to be married and is not particularly concerned about the identity of his future wife, though he would prefer her to be beautiful. ☐

d) Mr Wickham and Mr Darcy are delighted to renew their boyhood friendship. ☐

e) Elizabeth is unwilling to listen to damaging scandal from someone she has only just met. ☐

f) Jane is quick to believe that both Wickham and Darcy are as bad as each other. ☐

g) Mr Collins thinks that novels are shocking but has no hesitation playing cards. ☐

THINKING MORE DEEPLY ❓

❷ Write **one** or **two sentences** in response to each of these questions:

a) Why does Mr Collins admire Lady Catherine de Bourgh so much?

....

....

....

....

b) What makes Wickham so immediately attractive?

....

....

....

....

c) What does Mr Bennet think of Mr Collins?

....

....

....

....

EXAM PREPARATION: WRITING ABOUT THE INHERITANCE SYSTEM

Reread from *'It is from my cousin'* to *'I shall not be the person to discourage him.'* (pp. 50–2)

Question: What does this extract tell you about women and property in Jane Austen's time?

Think about:

- The contrast between Mr and Mrs Bennet's attitudes
- Mr Collins's lack of concern for the daughters' feelings

❸ Complete this table:

Point/detail	Evidence	Effect or explanation
1: *Mrs Bennet is described as 'beyond the reach of reason' on the subject of the entail yet today's readers may agree with much of what she says.*	*'If I had been you, I should have tried long ago to do something or other about it.'*	*At this point in the novel the reader's sympathy is with Mr Bennet. Later it becomes obvious that he has been lazy in not saving for his daughters' future.*
2: *Mr Bennet is neither thoughtful nor sensitive in the way he announces Mr Collins's visit.*		
3: *Mr Collins reserves the power to reveal his plans at a moment to suit him.*		

❹ Write up **point 1** into a **paragraph** below, in your own words. Remember to include what you infer from the evidence, or the writer's effects:

....

....

....

....

....

❺ Now, choose **one** of your **other points** and write it out as another **paragraph** here:

....

....

....

....

....

....

PROGRESS LOG [tick the correct box]   Needs more work ☐   Getting there ☐   Under control ☐

Volume 1, Chapters 18–21: Unwanted attention

QUICK TEST ✔

❶ Choose the correct answer to **finish the statement** and tick the box:

a) When she arrives at the Netherfield ball Elizabeth is particularly looking forward to dancing with:

Mr Collins ☐   Mr Darcy ☐   Mr Wickham ☐

b) Mary's performance on the piano is embarrassing and is made worse by comments from:

Miss Bingley ☐   Mr Bennet ☐   Mr Darcy ☐

c) When Elizabeth rejects Mr Collins's proposal he assumes this is because she:

hopes for a better offer ☐   doesn't love him ☐   is following female convention ☐

d) When Mr Collins realises that Elizabeth means what she says:

he respects her honesty ☐   he is distraught ☐   his pride is hurt ☐

e) Jane is upset by Caroline Bingley's letter because she realises that Caroline:

is not a true friend ☐   wants her brother to marry Miss Darcy ☐
is unlikely to write frequent letters ☐

THINKING MORE DEEPLY ❓

❷ Write **one** or **two sentences** in response to each of these questions:

a) How does Darcy react when Elizabeth mentions Wickham?

....

....

....

....

b) How does Mrs Bennet embarrass Elizabeth at the Netherfield ball?

....

....

....

....

c) Why is Mr Bennet's library important to him?

....

....

....

....

EXAM PREPARATION: WRITING ABOUT GENDER AND POWER

Reread from *'You must give me leave to flatter myself, my dear cousin'* to *'the affection and coquetry of an elegant female'* (p. 91).

Question: What does this scene between Mr Collins and Elizabeth tell us about gender and power?

Think about:

- Mr Collins's view of himself and his reasons for wanting to marry
- Elizabeth's heartfelt eloquence

❸ Complete this table:

Point/detail	Evidence	Effect or explanation
1: *Mr Collins tells Elizabeth that no one else will want to marry her as she has so little money.*	*'Your portion is unhappily so small that it will in all likelihood undo the effects of your loveliness'*	*Not only is this unromantic and insulting, it also highlights how little power women with no money of their own had over their futures.*
2: *In contrast to Mr Collins's pomposity, Elizabeth's speech is balanced, intelligent and clear.*		
3: *Elizabeth decides she must ask her father for help if Mr Collins will not listen to her.*		

❹ Write up **point 1** into a **paragraph** below, in your own words. Remember to include what you infer from the evidence, or the writer's effects:

....

....

....

....

....

❺ Now, choose **one** of your **other points** and write it out as another **paragraph** here:

....

....

....

....

....

....

PROGRESS LOG [tick the correct box]   Needs more work ☐   Getting there ☐   Under control ☐

Volume 1, Chapters 22–3: Mr Collins achieves his purpose

QUICK TEST

❶ Complete this **gap-fill** paragraph, adding the **correct or suitable information**:

The Lucas family are ……………………….. when Mr Collins asks their permission to marry

Charlotte. She is already ………………………… years old and is neither pretty nor rich. Marriage

to Mr Collins will give her her own ……………………………. and then, when Mr Bennet dies, she will

be able to move into …………………………. . Charlotte's marriage will make it easier for her

younger ………………………….. to attend social occasions and try to attract husbands for

themselves. It also means that her ……………………………. won't need to support her when their

father dies. Charlotte herself is prepared to overlook all Mr Collins's shortcomings for the sake of

…………………………. . She is only worried about losing …………………………. friendship.

THINKING MORE DEEPLY **?**

❷ Write **one** or **two sentences** in response to each of these questions:

a) Why is Elizabeth so shocked by Charlotte's decision?

....

....

....

....

b) What explanation does Charlotte give?

....

....

....

....

c) How well does Elizabeth manage her speech and reactions?

....

....

....

....

EXAM PREPARATION: WRITING ABOUT THE PATTERN OF EVENTS A02

Remind yourself of the themes and events of the opening chapter and compare it with the situation at the end of this first volume.

Question: What has changed in the course of Volume 1 and what remains the same?

Think about:

- Arrivals and departures
- How these relate to the themes of marriage and money

❸ Complete this table:

Point/detail	Evidence	Effect or explanation
1: *In Chapter 1, Mrs Bennet announced Bingley's arrival and raised hopes of marriage. She is distraught now he has left.*	*Initially, Mrs Bennet said: 'What a fine thing for our girls!'* *Now she is 'really in a most pitiable state'.*	*The focus on Mrs Bennet keeps the tone satirical. Austen highlights her inconsistency and self-delusion instead of focusing directly on Jane's heartbreak.*
2: *The balance of power between Mrs Bennet and Lady Lucas has shifted.*		
3: *Mrs Bennet's selfishness makes Jane's situation even more painful.*		

❹ Write up **point 1** into a **paragraph** below, in your own words. Remember to include what you infer from the evidence, or the writer's effects:

....

....

....

....

....

❺ Now, choose **one** of your **other points** and write it out as another **paragraph** here:

....

....

....

....

....

....

PROGRESS LOG [tick the correct box] Needs more work ☐ Getting there ☐ Under control ☐

Volume 2, Chapters 1–3: Disappointment for Jane

QUICK TEST

❶ From the list of names, identify which character is being **referred to**. Write the name next to each quotation.

Mr Bingley   **Miss Bingley**   **Mr Collins**   **Mr Gardiner**

Mrs Gardiner   **Charlotte Lucas**   **Mr Wickham**

a) Narrator: 'that easiness of temper [that] now made <u>him</u> the slave of his designing friends.' (p. 111)   ....

b) Jane: 'Remember that <u>she</u> is one of a large family; that as to fortune is it a most eligible match' (p. 113).   ....

c) Elizabeth: '[<u>He</u>] is a pompous, narrow-minded, silly man' (p. 113).   ....

d) Mr Bennet: '[<u>He</u>] is a pleasant fellow, and would jilt you creditably.' (p. 115)   ....

e) Narrator: '[<u>He</u>] was a sensible, gentlemanlike man' (p. 116).   ....

f) Narrator: '[<u>She</u>] was an amiable, intelligent, elegant woman' (p. 116).   ....

g) Jane: '[<u>She</u>] did not return my visit until yesterday' (p. 123).   ....

THINKING MORE DEEPLY ❓

❷ Write **one** or **two sentences** in response to each of these questions:

a) Why does Elizabeth think Jane is 'too good' (p. 112)?

....
....
....
....

b) What does Mrs Bennet complain about to Mrs Gardiner?

....
....
....
....

c) What does Elizabeth think of Charlotte's first letters home after her marriage?

....
....
....
....

Reread Jane's letter to Elizabeth (pp. 123–4).

Question: What has Jane learned about Miss Bingley and how has she learned it?

Think about:

- The importance of correct social behaviour
- The tone of the letter

❸ Complete this table:

Point/detail	Evidence	Effect or explanation
1: *Unlike Elizabeth, Jane had continued to trust Miss Bingley's friendship even after Mr Bingley had rejected her.*	*'I confess myself to have been entirely deceived'.*	*'Confess' and 'entirely deceived' are strong words. Jane is kind but not stupid. Once the evidence is clear she does not hesitate to admit her mistakes.*
2: *Jane judges Miss Bingley on her failure to write or return calls and on her behaviour when she visits.*		
3: *This letter gives insight into Jane's mind as she struggles to understand how she has misread the situation.*		

❹ Write up **point 1** into a **paragraph** below, in your own words. Remember to include what you infer from the evidence, or the writer's effects:

....

....

....

....

....

❺ Now, choose **one** of your **other points** and write it out as another **paragraph** here:

....

....

....

....

....

....

PROGRESS LOG [tick the correct box]   Needs more work ☐   Getting there ☐   Under control ☐

Volume 2, Chapters 4–5: To Hunsford Parsonage

QUICK TEST ✔

❶ Which of these are **TRUE** statements and which are **FALSE**? Write 'T' or 'F' in the boxes:

a) Mr Bennet is so upset at the thought of Elizabeth being away in Kent that he tells her to write to him and almost promises to answer her letters. ☐

b) Charlotte's sister, Maria Lucas, is a thoughtful, serious-minded young woman. ☐

c) Mr and Mrs Gardiner invite Elizabeth to join them on a seaside holiday in the summer. ☐

d) Charlotte is delighted that Elizabeth has come to visit her. ☐

e) Charlotte doesn't like Mr Collins spending too much time in the garden as it takes him away from her. ☐

f) Mr Collins is able to tell his visitors how many fields they can see and how many trees are in every clump. ☐

g) Elizabeth is interested in Miss de Bourgh as she believes she may be Mr Darcy's future wife. ☐

THINKING MORE DEEPLY ❓

❷ Write **one** or **two sentences** in response to each of these questions:

a) What is Mrs Gardiner's attitude to her two older nieces?

....

....

....

....

b) What does Elizabeth notice about the way Charlotte manages her home and her married life?

....

....

....

....

c) How do the Sir William and Maria Lucas react to Miss de Bourgh's visit?

....

....

....

....

EXAM PREPARATION: WRITING ABOUT CHARACTERS

Reread Elizabeth's first impressions of Hunsford Parsonage (pp. 129–31).

Question: How does Austen present the marriage of Charlotte and Mr Collins?

Think about:

- the portrayal of Mr Collins
- Elizabeth's observation of Charlotte

❸ Complete this table:

Point/detail	Evidence	Effect or explanation
1: *Mr Collins is as pompous and conceited in his own home as he is elsewhere. Marriage has not changed this.*	*'Elizabeth was prepared to see him in his glory'.*	*Mr Collins enjoys showing off his home and surroundings. He wants Elizabeth to recognise all that she has missed.*
2: *Austen suggests that Charlotte controls her true feelings.*		
3: *Charlotte finds pleasure in her housekeeping when Mr Collins is not around.*		

❹ Write up **point 1** into a **paragraph** below, in your own words. Remember to include what you infer from the evidence, or the writer's effects:

....

....

....

....

....

❺ Now, choose **one** of your **other points** and write it out as another **paragraph** here:

....

....

....

....

....

....

PROGRESS LOG [tick the correct box]   Needs more work ☐   Getting there ☐   Under control ☐

Volume 2, Chapters 6–10: Rosings Park

❶ Choose the correct answer to **finish the statement** and tick the box:

a) As they prepare to dine with Lady Catherine, Mr Collins is anxious that his guests will be:

overexcited ☐   overdressed ☐   overpowered ☐

b) Elizabeth finds Lady Catherine's questions about her family:

kindly ☐   condescending ☐   intrusive ☐

c) When Mr Darcy and Colonel Fitzwilliam arrive to stay with Lady Catherine they are quick to:

organise a ball ☐   call at Hunsford Parsonage ☐   invite Mr Collins to come fishing ☐

d) When the Hunsford Parsonage party is invited to spend the evening at Rosings, Colonel Fitzwilliam and Elizabeth discuss:

music ☐   politics ☐   landscape gardening ☐

e) When Mr Darcy calls at Hunsford Parsonage he:

takes an interest in Charlotte's housekeeping ☐   sits in silence ☐
listens to Mr Collins's sermons ☐

THINKING MORE DEEPLY ?

❷ Write **one** or **two sentences** in response to each of these questions:

a) What are Elizabeth's first impressions of Rosings?

b) How does Mr Darcy react to Elizabeth's piano playing?

c) What does Colonel Fitzwilliam say to Elizabeth about marriage and why?

EXAM PREPARATION: WRITING ABOUT LADY CATHERINE

Reread from *'Very few days passed'* to *'beyond the reach of Lady Catherine's curiosity'* (pp. 140–1).

Question: What role does Lady Catherine play in her neighbourhood?

Think about:

- Lady Catherine's actions
- The effect she has

❸ Complete this table:

Point/detail	Evidence	Effect or explanation
1: *When Lady Catherine visits Hunsford she assumes the authority to interfere in the minutest details of daily life.*	'She examined [. . .] their work, and advised them to do it differently.'	We can see the use of the word 'advised' as ironic as Lady Catherine has very strong views and expects to be obeyed.
2: *Lady Catherine is economically powerful.*		
3: *There is little to do at the Parsonage (except visit Rosings) but Elizabeth escapes Lady Catherine's company when she can.*		

❹ Write up **point 1** into a **paragraph** below, in your own words. Remember to include what you infer from the evidence, or the writer's effects:

....
....
....
....
....

❺ Now, choose **one** of your **other points** and write it out as another **paragraph** here:

....
....
....
....
....

PROGRESS LOG [tick the correct box]   Needs more work ☐   Getting there ☐   Under control ☐

Volume 2, Chapter 11: Darcy proposes

QUICK TEST

❶ Complete this **gap-fill** paragraph, adding the **correct or suitable information**:

The timing of Mr Darcy's .... proposal is especially unfortunate for

him. In literary terms it is an example of narrative .... Elizabeth has

just been told by .... of the part Darcy played in preventing Bingley's

.... to Jane. She is extremely upset by this so has stayed behind in

the parsonage while the others have gone to dine at .... To make

matters worse she has been rereading all the .... that Jane has sent her

since she has been away. Elizabeth can see Jane is not .... and therefore

becomes even more distressed herself. She hears the door bell and a few moments later

.... walks into the room.

THINKING MORE DEEPLY ❓

❷ Write **one** or **two sentences** in response to each of these questions:

a) What does Darcy's body language convey about his feelings?

....

....

....

....

b) What are Elizabeth's initial reactions?

....

....

....

....

c) What reasons does she give for her refusal?

....

....

....

....

EXAM PREPARATION: WRITING ABOUT THE THEME OF PRIDE

Reread from *'And this is all the reply I am to have'* to *'whose condition in life is so decidedly beneath my own'* (pp. 158–60).

Question: How is this scene related to the novel's overall theme of pride?

Think about:

- Darcy's surprise
- His objections to Elizabeth's family

❸ Complete this table:

Point/detail	Evidence	Effect or explanation
1: *Darcy's immediate reaction is to accuse Elizabeth of rudeness.*	*He asks: 'Why, with so little endeavour at civility, I am thus rejected'?*	*The reader will by now have noticed that Darcy always retreats into arrogance when he is upset. He speaks stiffly and this begins to anger Elizabeth.*
2: *Elizabeth's pride is also hurt and she accuses Darcy of rudeness in the language of his proposal.*		
3: *Darcy finally responds by telling Elizabeth exactly what he thinks of her family.*		

❹ Write up **point 1** into a **paragraph** below, in your own words. Remember to include what you infer from the evidence, or the writer's effects:

....

....

....

....

....

❺ Now, choose **one** of your **other points** and write it out as another **paragraph** here:

....

....

....

....

....

....

PROGRESS LOG [tick the correct box]   Needs more work ☐   Getting there ☐   Under control ☐

Volume 2, Chapters 12–13: A turning point for Elizabeth

QUICK TEST

❶ In relation to Mr Darcy's letter to Elizabeth, identify which character is being **referred to** from the list of names below. Write the name next to each quotation. Use each name at least once.

Mr Darcy   **Jane Bennet**   **Mr Wickham**   **Georgiana Darcy**

a) Narrator: 'With a strong prejudice against every thing <u>he</u> might say, [Elizabeth] began his account of what had happened.' (p. 169)   ....

b) Darcy: '<u>Her</u> look and manners were open, cheerful and engaging as ever, but without any symptom of peculiar regard.' (p. 163)   ....

c) Darcy: '<u>His</u> studying the law was a mere pretence, and being now free from all restraint, his life was a life of idleness and dissipation.' (p. 167)   ....

d) Darcy: '<u>She</u> was persuaded to believe herself in love, and consent to an elopement. She was then but fifteen' (pp. 167–8).   ....

e) Narrator: '[Elizabeth] could see <u>him</u> instantly before her, in every charm of air and address.' (p. 171)   ....

THINKING MORE DEEPLY ?

❷ Write **one** or **two sentences** in response to each of these questions:

a) What is the tone of Darcy's letter?

....

....

....

....

b) What does Darcy say that he noticed or learned during the Netherfield ball?

....

....

....

....

c) How does Elizabeth react as she reads?

....

....

....

....

EXAM PREPARATION: WRITING ABOUT ELIZABETH'S CHANGE OF HEART

Reread from *'How differently did every thing now appear'* to *'Till this moment, I never knew myself.'* (pp. 171–3)

Question: How does Austen help the reader share Elizabeth's thoughts and reactions?

Think about:

- The specific mistakes Elizabeth has made
- The way these are presented (style of writing)

❸ Complete this table:

Point/detail	Evidence	Effect or explanation
1: *Elizabeth is using her intellect and sense of fairness to think back and reassess the new evidence concerning Wickham.*	*'Every lingering struggle in his favour grew fainter and fainter'.*	*The word 'struggle' reveals Elizabeth's awareness that she wanted to think well of Wickham for emotional reasons but now she cannot.*
2: *The long first paragraph of this extract is expressed in formal language, almost like a summing up.*		
3: *The style of writing shifts to express Elizabeth's emotional response.*		

❹ Write up **point 1** into a **paragraph** below, in your own words. Remember to include what you infer from the evidence, or the writer's effects:

....
....
....
....
....

❺ Now, choose **one** of your **other points** and write it out as another **paragraph** here:

....
....
....
....
....

PROGRESS LOG [tick the correct box]   Needs more work ☐   Getting there ☐   Under control ☐

Volume 2, Chapters 14–19: Discontent at Longbourn

QUICK TEST ✓

1 Which of these are **TRUE** statements and which are **FALSE**? Write 'T' or 'F' in the boxes:

a) Elizabeth longs to return home so she can tell her family all that has occurred. ☐

b) Mr Collins is glad to have been able to introduce Elizabeth to very superior society. ☐

c) Mr Wickham is about to marry Miss King, an heiress. ☐

d) Lydia wants Jane and Elizabeth to walk into Meryton as soon as they arrive home but Elizabeth refuses. ☐

e) Mr Bennet firmly refuses to allow Lydia to go to Brighton. ☐

f) Kitty Bennet cannot enter Meryton without bursting into tears for two or three weeks after the regiment has left. ☐

THINKING MORE DEEPLY ?

2 Write **one** or **two sentences** in response to each of these questions:

a) How does Lydia greet her older sisters and Maria Lucas on their return?

....

....

....

....

b) How does Jane respond to Elizabeth's revelations about Wickham?

....

....

....

....

c) How does Elizabeth feel as she sets out on her holiday with the Gardiners?

....

....

....

....

EXAM PREPARATION: WRITING ABOUT LYDIA'S EFFECT ON HER FAMILY A01

Reread from *'The rapture of Lydia'* to *'tenderly flirting with at least six officers at once'* (pp. 190–2).

Question: How do Lydia, Elizabeth and Mr Bennet react to Lydia's invitation to Brighton?

Think about:

● Lydia's behaviour and expectations
● Elizabeth's conversation with her father

❸ Complete this table:

Point/detail	Evidence	Effect or explanation
1: *Lydia's behaviour is typically self-centred, insensitive and physically wild.*	*'Wholly inattentive to her sister's feelings, Lydia flew about the house'.*	*The narrator's observation that Lydia is 'wholly inattentive' emphasises her lack of sympathy for Kitty. The strong verbs (e.g. 'flew') express her uncontrolled energy.*
2: *Elizabeth is aware of the way Lydia's inappropriate behaviour affects the whole family.*		
3: *Mr Bennet's response shows his affection for Elizabeth but also his laziness.*		

❹ Write up **point 1** into a **paragraph** below, in your own words. Remember to include what you infer from the evidence, or the writer's effects:

....
....
....
....
....

❺ Now, choose **one** of your **other points** and write it out as another **paragraph** here:

....
....
....
....
....
....

PROGRESS LOG [tick the correct box]　　Needs more work ☐　　Getting there ☐　　Under control ☐

Volume 3, Chapters 1–3: Pemberley and its inhabitants

QUICK TEST ✔

❶ Choose the correct answer to **finish the statement** and tick the box:

a) The housekeeper at Pemberley describes Darcy as:

a proud ill-natured boy ☐   approachable and generous to the poor ☐   a wild young man ☐

b) Elizabeth and Darcy first encounter each other at Pemberley:

by accident ☐   in a formal call ☐   at the inn ☐

c) On first meeting Georgiana Darcy, Elizabeth realises that she is:

very accomplished ☐   proud ☐   extremely shy ☐

d) As soon as Elizabeth has left the room Caroline Bingley begins criticising her for her:

piano-playing ☐   tanned complexion ☐   choice of reading ☐

e) When they return to the inn Mrs Gardiner and Elizabeth talk about everything except:

Mr Darcy ☐   Miss Darcy ☐   Miss Bingley ☐

THINKING MORE DEEPLY ?

❷ Write **one** or **two sentences** in response to each of these questions:

a) How do Elizabeth's first impressions of Pemberley compare with her first impressions of Rosings?

....

....

....

....

b) What does the timing of Georgiana's visit suggest?

....

....

....

....

c) Why might people assume that Georgiana Darcy is proud?

....

....

....

EXAM PREPARATION: WRITING ABOUT KEY MOMENTS

Reread from *'Whilst wandering on in this slow manner, they were again surprised'* to *'It is impossible that he should still love me.'* (pp. 208–9)

Question: What do we learn from this key moment in the novel?

Think about:

- Elizabeth's thoughts and feelings
- The way Austen presents the gap between what is said and what is thought

❸ Complete this table:

Point/detail	Evidence	Effect or explanation
1: *Elizabeth expects Darcy to avoid her.*	*'For a few moments, indeed, she felt he would probably strike into some other path.'*	*While Elizabeth's speech is hesitant, Darcy shows no hesitation in approaching her.*
2: *The themes of pride, family, gentlemanliness all come together at this point.*		
3: *Austen switches from straightforward narration to internal questioning by Elizabeth.*		

❹ Write up **point 1** into a **paragraph** below, in your own words. Remember to include what you infer from the evidence, or the writer's effects:

....
....
....
....
....

❺ Now, choose **one** of your **other points** and write it out as another **paragraph** here:

....
....
....
....
....
....
....

PROGRESS LOG [tick the correct box]   Needs more work ☐   Getting there ☐   Under control ☐

Volume 3, Chapters 4–6: Bad news

QUICK TEST

❶ Complete this **gap-fill** paragraph, adding the **correct or suitable information**:

Elizabeth has been expecting .... from Jane. Two arrive together and Elizabeth's first clue that all is not well at .... is Jane's unusually bad handwriting. From then matters grow rapidly worse. The first letter tells the shocking news that Lydia has eloped to .... with Wickham. Jane is struggling to think .... of everyone and says this must mean Wickham truly loves Lydia as he knows Mr Bennet won't be able to give her any .... The second letter, however, contains the information that Wickham and Lydia are probably in London and are not .... Jane begs Elizabeth and the Gardiners to return home as .... has collapsed and .... is angry but ineffective. .... leaps up and runs to the door. At that moment .... arrives.

THINKING MORE DEEPLY **?**

❷ Write **one** or **two sentences** in response to each of these questions:

a) What does Elizabeth think after Darcy has left the room?

....
....
....
....

b) What is on Mrs Bennet's mind when Elizabeth and the Gardiners arrive at Longbourn?

....
....
....
....

c) What does Mr Bennet do?

....
....
....
....

EXAM PREPARATION: WRITING ABOUT THE USE OF LETTERS

Read from *'Every day at Longbourn was now a day of anxiety'* to *'I am, dear Sir, &c. &c.'* (pp. 243–4)

Question: What is the effect of Mr Collins's letter arriving at this tense moment?

Think about:

- The way the letter is written
- The content of the letter

❸ Complete this table:

Point/detail	Evidence	Effect or explanation
1: *Austen uses the arrival or non-arrival of letters to express helplessness and suspense at Longbourn.*	*'The arrival of letters was the first grand object of every morning's impatience.'*	*We understand that it is letters from London that are expected by the anxious family. The arrival of a letter from Kent is therefore a surprise.*
2: *Mr Collins's letter is an unwelcome reminder of the scandal and its lasting damage to all the Bennets.*		
3: *Mr Collins pretends he is writing to sympathise but his letter is entirely negative and uncharitable.*		

❹ Write up **point 1** into a **paragraph** below, in your own words. Remember to include what you infer from the evidence, or the writer's effects:

....

....

....

....

❺ Now, choose **one** of your **other points** and write it out as another **paragraph** here:

....

....

....

....

....

PROGRESS LOG [tick the correct box]   Needs more work ☐   Getting there ☐   Under control ☐

Volume 3, Chapters 7–10: Marriage and money

QUICK TEST ✓

① From the list of names below, identify which character is being **referred to**. Write the name next to each quotation. (Some people may be referred to more than once.)

Mr Darcy **Lydia** **Mr Wickham** **Mr Bennet**

a) Mr Bennet: '[He's] a fool if he takes her with a farthing less than ten thousand pounds.' (p. 250) ....

b) Narrator: 'When the first transports of rage which had produced his activity in seeking her were over, <u>he</u> naturally returned to his former indolence.' (p. 254) ....

c) Narrator: '[Elizabeth] now began to comprehend that <u>he</u> was exactly the man, who, in disposition and talents would most suit her.' (p. 256) ....

d) Mrs Bennet: 'It was such a pity that [<u>she</u>] should be taken from the regiment where she was so well acquainted with everybody, and had so many favourites.' (p. 258) ....

e) Mr Gardiner: '<u>He</u> has given in all his debts; I hope at least he has not deceived us.' (pp. 257–8) ....

THINKING MORE DEEPLY ❓

② Write **one** or **two sentences** in response to each of these questions:

a) What does Mrs Gardiner say about Mr Darcy's involvement in Lydia's marriage settlement?

....

....

....

....

b) How do Jane and Elizabeth expect Lydia to behave when she and Wickham visit Longbourn after their marriage?

....

....

....

....

c) How does Lydia behave when she and Wickham visit Longbourn after their marriage?

....

....

....

....

EXAM PREPARATION: WRITING ABOUT MRS BENNET'S CHANGES OF MOOD A01

Reread from *'Mrs Bennet could hardly contain herself'* to *'to make merry at her wedding.'* (pp. 251–2)

Question: What does Mrs Bennet's excitement tell you about her values and principles?

Think about:

- Mrs Bennet's relationship with her neighbours
- Mrs Bennet's understanding of marriage

❸ Complete this table:

Point/detail	Evidence	Effect or explanation
1: *Mrs Bennet's reaction to Lydia's elopement has been to withdraw to her room. Now her mood swings to wild excitement.*	*'I will go to Meryton […] and tell the good, good news to my sister Philips.'*	*Mrs Bennet seems to assume that all the shocking circumstances will now be forgotten in the light of this 'good news'.*
2: *For Mrs Bennet, Lydia's marriage means clothes. She has no awareness of any sacrifice made by anyone else.*		
3: *Mrs Bennet sees marriage as an end in itself. She doesn't think about Lydia's future happiness or security.*		

❹ Write up **point 1** into a **paragraph** below, in your own words. Remember to include what you infer from the evidence, or the writer's effects:

....

....

....

....

....

❺ Now, choose **one** of your **other points** and write it out as another **paragraph** here:

....

....

....

....

....

PROGRESS LOG [tick the correct box]   Needs more work ☐   Getting there ☐   Under control ☐

Volume 3, Chapters 11–15: Welcome and unwelcome visitors

QUICK TEST ✓

❶ Which of these are **TRUE** statements and which are **FALSE**? Write 'T' or 'F' in the boxes:

a) Jane Bennet and her mother have many contented conversations about Mr Bingley's expected return to Netherfield. ☐

b) Elizabeth realises at once how pleased Mr Darcy is to see her again. ☐

c) Mrs Bennet is delighted with the success of her dinner, Jane's beauty and the plainness of Mrs Long's nieces. ☐

d) Mr Bingley is invited to go shooting with Mr Bennet. ☐

e) Lady Catherine arrives to announce her daughter's official engagement to Mr Darcy. ☐

f) Elizabeth assures Lady Catherine that she will always be welcome at Pemberley. ☐

g) Mr Bennet is surprised when Elizabeth doesn't laugh at Mr Collins's letter about Mr Darcy. ☐

THINKING MORE DEEPLY ?

❷ Write **one** or **two sentences** in response to each of these questions:

a) How does Mrs Bennet make Elizabeth feel a 'misery of shame' when Darcy and Bingley come to call?

....

....

....

....

b) How does Jane behave when Bingley finally proposes to her?

....

....

....

....

c) How does Lady Catherine behave when she arrives at Longbourn?

....

....

....

....

EXAM PREPARATION: WRITING ABOUT AUSTEN'S USE OF HUMOUR

Reread from *'Elizabeth tried to join in her father's pleasantry'* to *'she might have fancied too much'* (pp. 300–1).

Question: How does Mr Bennet's sense of humour affect Elizabeth in this scene?

Think about:

- Their relationship as father and daughter
- The role of the narrator

❸ Complete this table:

Point/detail	Evidence	Effect or explanation
1: *Elizabeth's relationship with her father has always been close as they share a sense of humour. On this occasion it is different.*	*'Never had his wit been directed in a manner so little agreeable to her.'*	*The emphasis is on 'never'. Austen also shows Elizabeth's struggle to 'force' a 'reluctant' smile. We may wonder why she cannot confide in her father.*
2: *Mr Bennet is an intelligent man and loves Elizabeth but his view of the world is misguided.*		
3: *Austen shows us that Elizabeth is suffering from self-doubt. She wonders if her father is right when he speaks of Darcy's lack of interest in her.*		

❹ Write up **point 1** into a **paragraph** below, in your own words. Remember to include what you infer from the evidence, or the writer's effects:

....

....

....

....

....

❺ Now, choose **one** of your **other points** and write it out as another **paragraph** here:

....

....

....

....

....

PROGRESS LOG [tick the correct box]   Needs more work ☐   Getting there ☐   Under control ☐

Volume 3, Chapters 16–19: True love and marriage at last

QUICK TEST ✔

❶ Choose the correct answer to **finish the statement** and tick the box:

a) Darcy tells Elizabeth that he paid for Lydia's wedding because he:

likes the Gardiners ☐   loves Elizabeth ☐   feels guilty about Wickham ☐

b) Elizabeth explains that the letter Darcy wrote after she first rejected him:

was burned in Charlotte's fire ☐   immediately changed her mind ☐
challenged her prejudices ☐

c) Mr Bennet tells Elizabeth that he is afraid of her marrying:

without money ☐   without respect ☐   without new clothes ☐

d) Elizabeth did not answer Mrs Gardiner's letter at once because she was afraid that her aunt:

misunderstood her relationship with Darcy ☐   disapproved of the relationship ☐
would agree with Lady Catherine ☐

e) When Elizabeth teases Darcy after they are married, Georgiana reacts to this behaviour with:

hilarity ☐   disapproval ☐   astonishment ☐

THINKING MORE DEEPLY ?

❷ Write **one** or **two sentences** in response to each of these questions:

a) How easy is it for unmarried men and women in the novel to spend time together in private?

....

....

....

b) How does Jane respond to Elizabeth's news?

....

....

....

....

c) What do we learn about the younger Bennet sisters at the end of the novel?

....

....

....

EXAM PREPARATION: WRITING ABOUT MR DARCY'S CHARACTER **A01**

Reread from *'I cannot so easily be reconciled to myself'* to *'my anger soon began to take a proper direction'* (pp. 304–6).

Question: How does Austen help the reader understand how Darcy's character has changed?

Think about:

- How other people perceive Darcy's pride
- His own increased self-knowledge

❸ Complete this table:

Point/detail	Evidence	Effect or explanation
1: *At the start of the novel people assumed Darcy was proud because of his appearance and lack of conversation. Now he is able to speak for himself.*	*'I have been a selfish being all my life, in practice, though not in principle.'*	*For the first time, Austen reveals Darcy's inner thoughts and feelings about his 'life'.*
2: *Darcy explains that part of his pride has come from a solitary, overprotected childhood.*		
3: *Darcy is generous in his gratitude to Elizabeth for making him change.*		

❹ Write up **point 1** into a **paragraph** below, in your own words. Remember to include what you infer from the evidence, or the writer's effects:

....
....
....
....
....

❺ Now, choose **one** of your **other points** and write it out as another **paragraph** here:

....
....
....
....
....
....

PROGRESS LOG [tick the correct box]   Needs more work ☐   Getting there ☐   Under control ☐

Practice task

❶ First, **read** this **exam-style** task:

Read from: *'Allowing for the common demands of the game, Mr Wickham was therefore at leisure to talk to Elizabeth'* to *'but the delicacy of it prevented farther enquiry.'* (Vol. 1, Ch. 16, pp. 63–5)

Question: How does Elizabeth's misjudged first impression of Wickham contribute to the theme of pride and prejudice?

❷ Begin by circling the **key words** in the **question** above.

❸ Now, complete this table, noting down **3–4 key points** with **evidence** and the **effect** created:

Point	Evidence/quotation	Effect or explanation

❹ **Draft your response.** Use the space below for your first paragraph(s) and then continue onto a sheet of paper.

Start: *When Elizabeth recalls this first conversation between herself and Wickham she realises how wrong it had been …*

PROGRESS LOG [tick the correct box]   Needs more work ☐   Getting there ☐   Under control ☐

Who's who?

Look at these drawings and **complete** the **name** of each of the characters shown.

a) Fitzwilliam

....

b) Charles

....

c) Lady ....

de ....

d) George

....

e) Mr ....

f) Mrs ....

g) William

....

h) Charlotte

....

i) J.....................

Bennet

j) E.....................

Bennet

Elizabeth Bennet

❶ Look at these statements about Elizabeth. For each one, decide whether it is **True [T], False [F]** or whether there is **Not Enough Evidence [NEE]** to decide:

a) When we first meet Elizabeth her father describes her as
   'a young lady of deep reflection'.   [T] [F] [NEE]

b) Her immediate dislike of Miss Bingley and Mrs Hurst is proved correct.   [T] [F] [NEE]

c) At first she is not physically attracted by Mr Darcy.   [T] [F] [NEE]

d) She regrets her refusal of Mr Collins because she knows how much
   acceptance would mean to her mother and sisters.   [T] [F] [NEE]

e) She is overawed by the grandeur of Rosings Park.   [T] [F] [NEE]

f) She is secretly attracted to Colonel Fitzwilliam.   [T] [F] [NEE]

g) Her first impression on meeting shy Miss Darcy is sympathetic and
   understanding.   [T] [F] [NEE]

❷ Complete these **statements** about Elizabeth:

a) *Elizabeth laughs at her friend Charlotte's rational approach to marriage because she can't*
   believe that Charlotte would ever ... .

   ....

b) *In Volume 1, Chapter 11, when Mr Darcy accuses Elizabeth of being too ready to joke about*
   people she defends herself by saying that she only laughs at ... .

   ....

c) *Elizabeth explains to Colonel Fitzwilliam and Mr Darcy in Volume 2, Chapter 8 that her*
   performance on the piano is not as good as it could be because ... .

   ....

d) *When she first hears of the crisis over Lydia's elopement Elizabeth longs to be*
   at home so that she can help Jane ... .

   ....

❸ Using your **own judgment**, put a mark along this line to show **Jane Austen's**
overall presentation of Elizabeth:

Totally unsympathetic	A little sympathetic	Quite sympathetic	Very sympathetic
❶	❷	❸	❹

PROGRESS LOG [tick the correct box]   Needs more work ☐   Getting there ☐   Under control ☐

Mr Fitzwilliam Darcy

❶ Without checking the book, write down from memory at least **two pieces of information** we are told about Mr Darcy in each of these areas:

His background and manner	1:
	2:
His behaviour and what he thinks or says about others	1:
	2:
His relationships	1:
	2:

❷ Now **check your facts**. Are you right? Look at the following pages:

- His background and manner: Vol. 1, Ch. 3, p. 7; Vol. 1, Ch. 4, p. 12
- His behaviour and what he thinks or says about others:
  Vol. 1, Ch. 18, p. 76; Vol. 2, Ch. 8, pp. 145–6
- His relationships: Vol. 1, Ch. 4, p. 12; Vol. 3, Ch. 1, p. 203

❸ What evidence can you find in Vol. 3, Ch. 1 that Darcy's general attitude has changed but his attraction towards Elizabeth has not?

Find **evidence** in the text and include **quotations**.

Evidence	Quotation
a) *Blushing is usually considered to be a sign of physical attraction.*	*'Their eyes instantly met, and the cheeks of each were overspread with the deepest blush.'*
b) *Darcy asks after the Bennet family.*	
c) *Darcy asks to be introduced to the Gardiners.*	
d) *Darcy asks to be allowed to introduce his sister to Elizabeth.*	

PROGRESS LOG [tick the correct box]   Needs more work ☐   Getting there ☐   Under control ☐

Jane Bennet

❶ In the bank of **adjectives** below, circle the ones you think best **describe** Jane Bennet:

beautiful	enthusiastic	modest	critical
kindly	even-tempered	excitable	
reserved	trusting	suspicious	sharp-tongued
calm	sensitive	cynical	
self-centred	discreet	caring	loving

❷ Now add a **page reference** from your copy of the novel beside each circle showing where evidence can be found to **support** that **adjective**.

❸ Complete this **gap-fill** paragraph about Jane Bennet, adding the **correct or suitable information**:

Jane Bennet's .... with Caroline Bingley gives the reader some insight

into her .... Jane is a naturally .... person and

always thinks .... of other people where she can. She doesn't see that

Caroline is jealous and snobbish and assumes she is .... when she drops

hints that her brother prefers Miss Darcy. Jane however believes strongly in the importance

of good .... , so when Caroline fails to respond to her letters and calls

in London and then is deliberately rude, Jane begins to see her as she is. She is

honest in admitting to Elizabeth that she has been ....

❹ Using your **own judgement**, put a mark along this line to show **Jane Austen's overall presentation** of Jane Bennet.

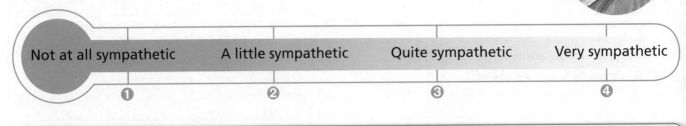

Not at all sympathetic	A little sympathetic	Quite sympathetic	Very sympathetic
❶	❷	❸	❹

PROGRESS LOG [tick the correct box]   Needs more work ☐   Getting there ☐   Under control ☐

Mr Charles Bingley

❶ Each of the character traits below could be applied to Mr Bingley. Working from memory, add points in the novel where you think these are shown, then find at least one quotation to back up each aspect.

Quality	Moment in novel	Quotation
a) Friendly		
b) Easy-going		
c) Modest		
d) Loving		

❷ Use some of the descriptive words from the bank at the bottom of the page to complete this **gap-fill** paragraph about Mr Bingley.

When Mr Bennet describes Jane and Bingley as being so '.............................'

and '.............................' that they are likely to be cheated by their servants

and to get into debt, Jane is shocked yet the reader will know that Mr Bennet's

teasing remarks have a kernel of truth. We have already seen Bingley's tendency

towards .... when leaving Netherfield for London and his

.... or even (in Elizabeth's opinion) .... in

yielding to his sisters' and Darcy's advice not to return. The narrator has told us of

his .... approach to buying or renting property and his

.... reliance on his housekeeper to make all the practical

arrangements. He is obviously .... as he provides a home for

both his sisters and agrees .... to Lydia's request for a ball.

business-like	*shrewdness*	*impulsive*	*obstinacy*	*unhesitatingly*
	weakness	*reluctantly*	*hastiness*	
complying	*thoughtfulness*	*casual*	*persuadability*	*generous*

PROGRESS LOG [tick the correct box]   Needs more work ☐   Getting there ☐   Under control ☐

Mr and Mrs Bennet

❶ Look at these statements about Mr and Mrs Bennet. For each one, decide whether it is **True [T]**, **False [F]** or whether there is **Not Enough Evidence [NEE]** to decide:

a) Mr and Mrs Bennet are a devoted and mutually supportive couple. [T] [F] [NEE]

b) Neither Mr nor Mrs Bennet has taken the trouble to save money. [T] [F] [NEE]

c) Mr Bennet was attracted to Mrs Bennet because of her good looks and liveliness. [T] [F] [NEE]

d) Mrs Bennet was attracted to Mr Bennet because of his good looks and liveliness. [T] [F] [NEE]

e) Mrs Bennet tells Elizabeth she will never speak to her again if she does not marry Mr Collins. [T] [F] [NEE]

f) Mr Bennet tells Elizabeth he will never speak to her again if she does not marry Mr Collins. [T] [F] [NEE]

g) Mr and Mrs Bennet's marriage becomes happier once most of their daughters are married. [T] [F] [NEE]

❷ Without checking the book, write down from memory at least **two pieces of information** we are told about the Bennet parents in each of these areas:

His and her general personality (using either your own or the narrator's words)	1: *Mr Bennet ...* 2: *Mrs Bennet ...*
His and her behaviour in public	1: 2:
Their relationship either day to day or in times of stress	1: 2:

❸ Now **check your facts**. Are you right? Look at the following pages:

- His and her general personality: Vol. 1, Ch. 1, p. 3
- His and her behaviour at the Netherfield ball: Vol. 1, Ch. 18, p. 84 (Mr Bennet) and pp. 82–3 (Mrs Bennet)
- Day to day: Vol. 1, Ch. 2, p. 5 (Mr Bennet teasing); Vol. 1, Ch. 1, p. 3 (Mrs Bennet's lack of understanding)
- Relationship in times of stress: Vol. 1, Ch. 20, p. 93–4 (Mr Bennet); Vol. 3, Ch. 4, p. 225 (Mrs Bennet)

PROGRESS LOG [tick the correct box]   Needs more work ☐   Getting there ☐   Under control ☐

Mr William Collins

❶ Each of the character traits below could be applied to Mr Collins. Working from memory, add points in the novel where you think these are shown, then find at least one quotation to back up each aspect.

Quality	Moment in novel	Quotation
a) Pomposity		
b) Apparent humility		
c) Actual conceit		
d) Unforgiving		

❷ Look at this quotation from Mr Collins (Vol. 1, Ch. 19, p. 91). Add further annotations to it, finding suitable adjectives from the bank at the bottom of the page and explaining how Austen's words help to convey Mr Collins's character.

'It does not appear to me that my hand is unworthy of your acceptance, or that the establishment I can offer would be other than highly desirable. My situation in life, my connections with the family of de Bourgh, and my relationship to your own, are circumstances highly in my favour; and you should take it into farther consideration that in spite of your manifold attractions, it is by no means certain that another offer of marriage may ever be made to you.'

self-centred – shown by the repetition of the word 'my'

self-centred	conceited	materialistic	bullying
ponderous	unintelligent	unsympathetic	unkind

PROGRESS LOG [tick the correct box]   Needs more work ☐   Getting there ☐   Under control ☐

Mr George Wickham

❶ In the bank of **adjectives** below, circle the ones you think best **describe** George Wickham:

charming	shy	good-looking	friendly	proud
polite	gentlemanlike	greedy	indiscreet	romantic
impulsive	mercenary	extravagant	vicious	idle
unscrupulous	vengeful		grateful	contrite

❷ Now add a **page reference** from your copy of the novel beside each circle, showing where evidence can be found to **support** that **adjective**.

❸ Complete this **gap-fill** paragraph about George Wickham, adding the **correct or suitable information**:

Wickham's quality of shamelessness is never more apparent than when he and Lydia

visit .... after their marriage. Jane, Elizabeth and Mr Bennet had

all expected him to appear .... or even apologetic. Instead the

couple arrive full of 'easy assurance' and expect to be as welcome as if nothing

.... had occurred. When Wickham is alone with ....

he tries once again to gain her sympathy for his misfortunes in the past and repeats

his allegations of cruel treatment by .... Once he realises that

she knows the truth he pretends to be gallant and .... but

never mentions the subject again. Mr Bennet describes him ironically as a

'fine fellow' who 'simpers, and ...., and makes love to

us all'.

❹ Using your **own judgement**, put a mark along this line to show **Jane Austen's overall presentation** of George Wickham:

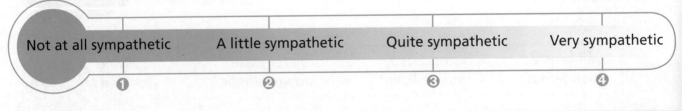

Charlotte Lucas

❶ Without checking the book, write down from memory at least **two pieces of information** we are told about Charlotte Lucas in each of these areas:

Her background, age and manner	1:
	2:
Her opinions and behaviour	1:
	2:
Her relationships	1:
	2:

❷ Now **check your facts**. Are you right? Look at the following pages:

- Her background, age and manner: Vol. 1, Ch. 5, p. 13
- Her opinions: Vol. 1, Ch. 5, p. 14
- Her tactful behaviour: Vol. 1, Ch. 20, p. 94–5
- Values her friendship with Elizabeth: Vol. 1, Ch. 22, p. 103
- Coping with Mr Collins: Vol. 2, Ch. 7 pp. 139–40

Lydia Bennet

❶ Each of the character traits below could be applied to Lydia Bennet. Working from memory, add points in the novel where you think these are shown, then find at least one quotation to back up each aspect.

Quality	Moment in the novel	Quotation
Overconfident		
Lively		
Attention-seeking		
Insensitive		

PROGRESS LOG [tick the correct box]   Needs more work ☐   Getting there ☐   Under control ☐

Caroline Bingley and Louisa Hurst

❶ Complete each statement about Caroline Bingley and Louisa Hurst, adding the **correct or suitable information**:

a) *Elizabeth's first impression of both Caroline Bingley and her sister Louisa is*

....

....

b) *Caroline and Louisa can be agreeable when they choose but are described by the narrator as* ....

....

c) *Caroline and Louisa prefer to forget that their fortunes* ....

....

d) *Caroline tries to ingratiate herself with Mr Darcy by* ....

....

e) *Caroline's jealous criticisms of Elizabeth to Mr Darcy finally result in* ....

....

....

Lady Catherine de Bourgh

❶ Look at these **adjectives** which could be used to describe Lady Catherine de Bourgh. **Circle** the qualities that **Mr Collins** sees in her (or she might claim for herself) and **underline** the qualities that **other people** (including the narrator) notice. A few words could be both circled and underlined:

generous	affable	proud	condescending	gracious
arrogant	conceited	dictatorial	insolent	charming
stately	authoritative	impertinent	self-centred	music-loving
musically-ignorant		interfering	frank	insulting

❷ Now add page references showing where evidence can be found to **support** each **adjective**.

PROGRESS LOG [tick the correct box]   Needs more work ☐   Getting there ☐   Under control ☐

Practice task

❶ First, **read** this **exam-style** task:

> Question: How is Georgiana Darcy presented by Jane Austen?
>
> Think about:
>
> - How other characters describe her
> - How she is described by the narrator when Elizabeth finally meets her

❷ Begin by circling the **key words** in the **question** above.

❸ Now complete this table, noting down **3–4 key points** with **evidence** and the **effect** created:

Point	Evidence/quotation	Effect or explanation

❹ **Draft your response**. Use the space below for your first paragraph(s) and then continue onto a sheet of paper.

Start: *When Elizabeth first meets Georgiana Darcy she realises at once that Georgiana is …*

....
....
....
....
....
....
....

PROGRESS LOG [tick the correct box]   Needs more work ☐   Getting there ☐   Under control ☐

Themes

QUICK TEST

❶ Complete this **gap-fill** paragraph about the theme of pride, adding the **correct or suitable information**:

Jane Austen offers the reader many .... on the theme of pride. The people at

the Meryton Assembly judge .... to be proud because he is reluctant to

.... or join in conversation. When the Bennets and the Lucases are discussing

him the following day Charlotte Lucas says Darcy has a .... to be proud because

of his good family and good income. She is presenting pride as something closer to

.... Arrogance, as exemplified by ...., is presented as a fault

and Darcy admits he has needed Elizabeth to cure him of it. Mr Collins, who appears so humble, is

far too .... to believe that Elizabeth does not find his proposal attractive,

whereas rich Mr Bingley's quality of .... is so extreme that he trusts Darcy's

opinion of Jane and not his own feelings for her.

❷ These comments by different characters suggest **themes** in the novel. From the list below, choose the best **abstract noun** (or **nouns**) to identify the theme (or themes) in each comment. Write the noun (or nouns) under each quotation:

a) **Elizabeth:** 'You make me laugh, Charlotte; but it is not sound. You know it is not sound, and that you would never act in this way yourself.' (Vol. 1, Ch. 6, p. 17)

....

b) **Lady Catherine:** 'Upon my word [...] you give your opinion very decidedly for so young a person. – Pray, what is your age?' (Vol. 2, Ch. 6, p. 138)

....

c) **Elizabeth:** 'And yet I meant to be uncommonly clever in taking so decided a dislike to him, without any reason.' (Vol. 2, Ch. 17, p. 186)

....

d) **Darcy:** 'I came to you without a doubt of my reception. You showed me how insufficient were all my pretensions to please a woman worthy of being pleased.' (Vol. 3, Ch. 16, p. 306)

....

prejudice	appearance	tragedy	manners	rejection
	pride	money	marriage	family

THINKING MORE DEEPLY

❸ Write **two** or **three sentences** to show how quotations a) and b) in Question 2 reveal a **theme** you identified. Include a comment on the **writer's effects**.

a) *Elizabeth's comment to Charlotte is linked to the theme of ...* ....

because ... .

....

....

....

Austen's effect is ... .

....

b) *Lady Catherine's remark is linked to the theme of ...* ....

because ... .

....

....

....

Austen's effect is ... .

....

❹ Complete each statement about the **theme** of **manners**.

a) *Darcy accuses various members of the Bennet family of a 'total want of propriety'. By 'propriety' he means ...* ....

....

....

....

b) *Good manners are linked to self-control and sensitivity to other people's feelings. Mrs Bennet lacks all of these. This means that she is ...* ....

....

....

....

c) *When Elizabeth's eyes are opened to Wickham's true character she uses the words 'impropriety' and 'indelicacy' because ...* ....

....

....

....

Part Four: Themes, Contexts and Settings

⑤ Write **one** or **two sentences** in response to each of these questions about the **themes of the novel**. Include a comment on the writer's effects.

a) When Elizabeth is telling Jane about Wickham's disgraceful treatment by Mr Darcy she says 'there was truth in his looks.' (Vol. 1, Ch. 17, p. 71) How does this conversation link to the theme of prejudice?

....

....

....

....

....

b) Which themes are introduced in the opening sentence of the novel and what does Austen's choice of words suggest?

....

....

....

....

....

⑥ Write **one** or **two sentences** to show how these comments reveal the speaker's attitude to the theme of family:

a) Elizabeth: 'She will, at sixteen, be the most determined flirt that ever made herself and her family ridiculous.' (Vol. 2, Ch. 18, p. 191)

....

....

....

....

....

b) Mr Collins: 'For who, as Lady Catherine condescendingly says, will ally themselves with such a family?' (Vol. 3, Ch. 6, p. 244)

....

....

....

....

....

Contexts

QUICK TEST ✔

❶ Choose the correct answer about the **context** of the novel and tick the box.

a) When was the novel first published?

1713 ☐   1813 ☐   1913 ☐

b) How would you refer to the period when it is set?

Tudor ☐   Postwar ☐   Regency ☐

c) How would you describe Jane Austen's social class (approximately)?

gentry ☐   middle class ☐   working class ☐

d) What was Jane Austen's father's profession?

clergyman ☐   farmer ☐   businessman ☐

e) How would you describe Austen's financial position while she was writing *Pride and Prejudice*?

wealthy ☐   starving ☐   dependent ☐

THINKING MORE DEEPLY ?

❷ Write **one** or **two sentences** in response to each of these questions:

a) In *Pride and Prejudice* what evidence do you see of England's war with France?

....
....
....
....

b) How important was reading in Austen's life and how is this shown in the novel?

....
....
....
....

c) What effect (if any) do you think Austen's gender is likely to have had on her success as a writer?

....
....
....
....

PROGRESS LOG [tick the correct box]   Needs more work ☐   Getting there ☐   Under control ☐

EXAM PREPARATION: WRITING ABOUT SOCIAL CLASS

Remind yourself of the scene in which Elizabeth and the Gardiners meet the housekeeper at Pemberley (Vol. 3, Ch. 1, pp. 201–5).

Question: Why is this scene significant?

❸ Complete this table:

Point/detail	Evidence	Effect or explanation
1: *Elizabeth is surprised by Mrs Reynolds's friendliness.*	'a respectable-looking elderly woman, much less fine and more civil than she had any notion of finding her'	*Mrs Reynolds's approachability is reassuring after the grandeur of the house and the park. This prepares the reader to see Pemberley as a family home.*
2: *Mrs Reynolds provides a first-hand account of Darcy as a child.*		
3: *Austen suggests that the housekeeper's opinions are solidly based and credible.*		

❹ Write up **point 1** into a **paragraph** below, in your own words.

....

....

....

....

....

❺ Now choose **one** of your **other points** and write it up as **another paragraph** here.

....

....

....

....

....

PROGRESS LOG [tick the correct box]   Needs more work ☐   Getting there ☐   Under control ☐

Settings

❶ Write down the names of the characters who live in each of the locations. Then give the number of the volume in which the setting is especially important.

Pemberley

Home of: ....

.... Volume: ....

Rosings

Home of: ....

.... Volume: ....

Hunsford Parsonage

Home of: ....

.... Volume: ....

Longbourn

Home of: ....

.... Volume: ....

Meryton

Home of: ....

.... Volume: ....

Netherfield Park

Home of: ....

.... Volume: ....

THINKING MORE DEEPLY

❷ Write **one** or **two sentences** in response to each of these questions about the **settings** of the novel. Include a comment on the **writer's effects**.

a) How does Charlotte manage her new home in Hunsford Parsonage?

....

....

....

....

b) What impression does Rosings Park make on visitors?

....

....

....

....

c) How do women achieve privacy in any of the houses?

....

....

....

....

❸ Pemberley is presented as an ideal location. Complete this table, giving some of its important features:

Point/detail	Evidence	Effect/explanation
1: *The setting combines natural beauty with discreet human management.*	*'She had never seen a place for which nature had done more, or where natural beauty had been so little counteracted by an awkward taste.'*	*We view Pemberley for the first time through Elizabeth's eyes. As well as revealing her personal feelings, this shows her appreciation for the Romantic movement in landscape.*
2: *The furnishing is favourably compared to Rosings. Things have been chosen for beauty and use.*		
3: *A big estate needs good management. Lady Catherine 'scolded' her tenants: Mr Darcy is kinder to his.*		

PROGRESS LOG [tick the correct box]   Needs more work ☐   Getting there ☐   Under control ☐

Practice task

❶ First, **read** this **exam-style** task:

Question: How does Jane Austen use characters' attitude to reading to tell us more about them. Answer this question with reference to at least three characters.

❷ Begin by circling the **key words** in the **question** above.

❸ Now, complete this table, noting down **3–4 key points** with **evidence** and the **effect** created:

Point	Evidence/quotation	Effect

❹ **Draft your response**. Use the space below for your first paragraph(s) and then continue onto a sheet of paper.

Start: *Jane Austen frequently uses her characters' attitude to books and reading to tell us more about them. Very often the effect is comic, as in this scene when …* ....

....

....

....

....

....

....

....

....

....

....

PROGRESS LOG [tick the correct box]   Needs more work ☐   Getting there ☐   Under control ☐

PART FIVE: FORM, STRUCTURE AND LANGUAGE

Form

❶ Choose the correct answer about the form of *Pride and Prejudice* to **finish the statement** and tick the box.

a) *Pride and Prejudice* was published in 1813 as:

a collection of letters ☐   a screenplay ☐   a novel ☐

b) In 1813 the majority of novels were:

sold at railway stations ☐   borrowed from circulating libraries ☐   most popular in paperback ☐

c) Jane Austen is known to have admired the novels of Samuel Richardson. These were:

epistolary novels ☐   comic novels ☐   Gothic novels ☐

d) Another form of reading that Austen is known to have enjoyed and which may have influenced *Pride and Prejudice* as a novel of manners was:

sermons ☐   epic poetry ☐   essays ☐

THINKING MORE DEEPLY ?

❷ Write **one** or **two sentences** in response to each of these questions:

a) What aspects of *Pride and Prejudice* identify it as a romantic novel?

....

....

....

....

b) What aspects of *Pride and Prejudice* identify it as a realistic novel?

....

....

....

....

c) What aspects of *Pride and Prejudice* identify it as a comic novel?

....

....

....

....

PROGRESS LOG [tick the correct box]   Needs more work ☐   Getting there ☐   Under control ☐

Structure

❶ Without checking the book, try to remember both the location of the following scenes and the volume in which they take place:

Scene	Location	Volume number
1: Elizabeth enjoys lively conversation and possible mutual attraction with George Wickham.		
2: Elizabeth and Charlotte discuss their different views of marriage.		
3: Mr Bennet warns Elizabeth against marriage without respecting her 'partner in life'.		
4: Elizabeth begs her father not to allow Lydia to go to Brighton.		
5: Mr Darcy finally loses patience with Caroline Bingley.		

THINKING MORE DEEPLY

❷ Write **one** or **two sentences** in response to each of these questions about **structure** and **plot**:

a) How does Austen use letters in her development of the plot?

....

....

....

....

b) Which pairs of characters are introduced together and what do these pairings tell us?

....

....

....

....

c) What device does Austen use to bind her characters and events together?

....

....

....

....

PROGRESS LOG [tick the correct box]   Needs more work ☐   Getting there ☐   Under control ☐

Language

❶ First **match** these **words/expressions** to their **meanings** without checking the novel:

Word/expression:	Meaning:
a) 'Michaelmas'	approachable
b) 'entail'	legal restriction on who can inherit a family's property
c) 'in his regimentals'	proper social conduct
d) 'mortification'	humiliation
e) 'propriety'	become a prostitute
f) 'affable'	in his uniform
g) 'come upon the town'	29 September, an annual quarter day for business transactions

❷ Now check the **words in context**. Look at the following pages. Do you want to change any of your answers?

a) p. 1 b) p. 21 c) p. 23 d) p. 75 e) p. 150 f) p. 199 g) p. 254

❸ For each of the **feelings** listed below, think of a moment in the novel when it is expressed. Find a **quotation** to back up each of your examples:

Feeling	Moment in the novel	Quotation
1: Bliss	*When Elizabeth and Darcy finally admit that they love each other and want to marry*	
2: Outrage		
3: Shock		

❹ Now **underline** the key words in the **quotation** that convey the **feeling**.

⑤ Read these comments and identify the speaker from the style of their speech and what they say. Choose the correct the name from the box below.

a) 'A house in town! Every thing that is charming! Three daughters married! Ten thousand a year!' (Vol. 3, Ch. 17, p. 314) ....

b) 'I never in my life saw any one so altered as she is since the winter. She is grown so brown and coarse!' (Vol. 3, Ch. 4, p. 222) ....

c) 'I will answer for it that he never cared three straws about her. Who *could* about such a nasty little freckled thing?' (Vol. 2, Ch. 16, p. 182) ....

d) 'There are few people in England, I suppose, who have more true enjoyment of music than myself, or a better natural taste. If I had ever learnt, I should have been a great proficient.' (Vol. 2, Ch. 8, p. 143) ....

e) 'As I must therefore conclude that you are not serious in your rejection of me, I shall choose to attribute it to your wish of increasing my love by suspense, according to the usual practice of elegant females.' (Vol. 1, Ch. 19, p. 91) ....

f) 'There is a mixture of servility and self-importance in his letter, which promises well. I am impatient to see him.' (Vol. 1, Ch. 13, p. 52) ....

g) 'Happiness in marriage is entirely a matter of chance.' (Vol. 1, Ch. 6, p. 17) ....

Mr Bennet	Mrs Bennet	Lydia Bennet	Mr Collins
Charlotte Lucas	Lady Catherine de Bourgh		Caroline Bingley

⑥ From the list below, identify the **technique** used and describe or explain **what it does**:

Example or quotation	Literary technique	Meaning/effect
1: 'One has got all the goodness, and the other all the appearance of it' (Vol. 2, Ch. 17, p. 186)		
2: 'You refuse to obey the claims of duty, honour, and gratitude.' (Vol. 3, Ch. 15, p. 296)		
3: 'Lady Lucas was enquiring [...] after the welfare and poultry of her eldest daughter' (Vol. 2, Ch. 16, p. 183)		

Use of concrete nouns	Balanced sentence	Rhetorical pattern of three

EXAM PREPARATION: WRITING ABOUT NARRATIVE VOICE (A02)

Reread from *'Elizabeth was prepared to see him in his glory'* to *'supposed he must be often forgotten'* (Vol. 2, Ch. 5, pp. 130–1).

Question: How does Jane Austen present events from Elizabeth's point of view?

Think about the use of:

- Concrete and abstract words
- Ironic tone
- Body language

7 Complete this table:

Technique	Example	Effect
1: *Use of abstract nouns*	'she was not able to gratify him with any sign of repentance'	The word 'repentance' is a strong word with a religious overtone which gives an ironic effect as it is so far from what she feels.
2: *Use of concrete nouns*		
3: *Use of unspoken communication*		

8 Write up **point 1** into a **paragraph** below, in your own words.

....

....

....

....

....

9 Now, choose **one** of your **other points** and write it up as **another paragraph** here:

....

....

....

....

....

....

PROGRESS LOG [tick the correct box]   Needs more work ☐   Getting there ☐   Under control ☐

Practice task

❶ First, read this **exam-style** task:

Question: Jane Austen described *Pride and Prejudice* as 'rather too light, and bright, and sparkling'. What is your impression of the overall style of the novel?

❷ Begin by circling the **key words** in the **question** above.

❸ Now, complete this table, noting down **3–4 key points** with **evidence** and the **effect** created:

Point	Evidence	Effect

❹ **Draft your response**. Use the space below for your first paragraph(s) and then continue onto a sheet of paper.

Start: *An ironic tone is characteristic of Austen's style as the narrator of 'Pride and Prejudice' and there is often a distance between what the narrator says and what she …*

....

....

....

....

....

....

....

PROGRESS LOG [tick the correct box]   Needs more work ☐   Getting there ☐   Under control ☐

Expressing and explaining ideas

❶ How well can you express your ideas about *Pride and Prejudice*? Look at this grid and tick the level you think you are currently at:

Level	How you respond	Writing skills	Tick
High	• You analyse the effect of specific words and phrases very closely (i.e. 'zooming in' on them and exploring their meaning). • You select quotations very carefully and you embed them fluently in your sentences. • You are persuasive and convincing in the points you make, often coming up with original ideas.	• You use a wide range of specialist terms (words like 'imagery'), excellent punctuation, accurate spelling, grammar, etc.	
Mid/ Good	• You analyse some parts of the text closely, but not all the time. • You support what you say with evidence and quotations, but sometimes your writing could be more fluent to read. • You make relevant comments on the text.	• You use a good range of specialist terms, generally accurate punctuation, usually accurate spelling, grammar, etc.	
Lower	• You comment on some words and phrases but often you do not develop your ideas. • You sometimes use quotations to back up what you say but they are not always well chosen. • You mention the effect of certain words and phrases but these are not always relevant to the task.	• You do not have a very wide range of specialist terms, but you use reasonably accurate spelling, punctuation and grammar.	

SELECTING AND USING QUOTATIONS

❷ Read these two samples from students' responses to a question about how Lydia is presented. Decide which of the three levels they fit best, i.e. **lower** (L), **mid** (M) or **high** (H).

Student A: *Austen presents Lydia as a character incapable of change. This is evident when she and Wickham return to Longbourn after their wedding. The reader has been given insight into how either Jane or Elizabeth would have felt but from the moment her voice is heard it is clear that Lydia has no self-doubt: 'Lydia was Lydia still.'*

Level: ☐   Why? ....

....

Student B: *Lydia is always cheerful as long as she gets her own way. She has no worries and when she comes back to Longbourn she is really pleased to see her family again. 'Lydia was Lydia still'.*

Level: ☐   Why? ....

....

*AO4 is assessed by OCR only.

ZOOMING IN – YOUR TURN!

Here is the first part of another student response. The student has picked a good quotation but hasn't 'zoomed in' on any particular words or phrases:

When Darcy is explaining to Elizabeth how he has changed and how grateful he is for this, he reminds her of the 'well applied' reproof she made to him: 'had you behaved in a more gentleman-like manner'. This shows that Darcy is genuinely sorry.

❸ Pick out one of the **words** or **phrases** the student has quoted and write a further sentence to complete the explanation:

The word/phrase '..' suggests that ....

....

....

EXPLAINING IDEAS

You need to be precise about the ways Jane Austen gets ideas across. This can be done by varying your use of verbs (not just using 'says' or 'means').

❹ Read this paragraph from a **mid-level** response to a question about Mr Bennet's relationship with his wife. Circle all the verbs that are repeated in the student's writing (not in the quotation):

Elizabeth says that her parents' marriage is neither satisfying nor admirable. The narrator says that they married because Mr Bennet was attracted by Mrs Bennet's 'appearance of good humour' as well as by her good looks. She says that when he discovered how shallow and ignorant his wife was he took refuge in his books and in secretly laughing at her. Austen says 'this is not the sort of happiness which a man would in general wish to owe to his wife'.

❺ Now choose some of the words in the bank below to replace your circled ones:

suggests	implies	tells us	presents	signals	asks
demonstrates	comments	states	explains	asserts	

❻ Rewrite your **high-level** version of the paragraph in full below. Remember to mention the **author by name** to show you understand that she is **making choices** in how she presents characters, themes and events.

....

....

....

....

....

....

....

PROGRESS LOG [tick the correct box]   Needs more work ☐   Getting there ☐   Under control ☐

Making inferences and interpretations

WRITING ABOUT INFERENCES

You need to be able to show you can read between the lines and make **inferences**, rather than just explain more explicit 'surface' meanings.

Here is an extract from one student's **high-level** response to a question about Jane Bennet and how she is presented:

Jane Bennet is presented as a character who is almost too good to be true but yet she remains human and sympathetic. At the end of Volume One Jane is suffering both from Bingley's desertion and from her mother's constant allusions to his absence. 'Oh! that my dear mother had more command of herself,' she says after what the narrator describes as a 'longer than usual irritation'. The very fact that Jane bursts out in this way suggests how sensitive she is and the depth of her pain.

❶ Look at the response carefully.
- **Underline** the simple point which explains what Jane does.
- **Circle** the sentence that develops the first point.
- **Highlight** the sentence that shows an inference and begins to explore wider interpretations.

INTERPRETING – YOUR TURN!

❷ Read the opening to this student response carefully and then **choose the sentence** from the list which shows **inference** and could lead to **a deeper interpretation**. Remember – interpreting is *not* guesswork!

Elizabeth's first sight of Anne de Bourgh is not encouraging. She considers Miss de Bourgh rude for keeping Charlotte standing outside in the cold; then other thoughts occur to her: 'She looks sickly and cross. – Yes, she will do for him very well. She will make him a very proper wife.' Elizabeth ...

a) *thinks of Miss de Bourgh marrying Mr Darcy because she is staying in the home of two newly married people.*

b) *is thinking of Mr Darcy at this moment because she is more attracted to him than she realises and he is there, unconsciously, in her mind.*

c) *thinks that Mr Darcy is bad tempered, so they will make a good match.*

❸ Now **complete** this **paragraph** about Jane, adding your own final sentence which makes inferences or explores wider interpretations:

Jane is consistently presented as a character who is too kind for her own good. In the crisis after Lydia's elopement she takes the entire burden on herself because 'Kitty is slight and delicate, and Mary studies so much, that her hours of repose should not be broken in on.' Elizabeth's description of Jane's obvious exhaustion implies that ... .

....

....

....

....

PROGRESS LOG [tick the correct box]   Needs more work ☐   Getting there ☐   Under control ☐

Writing about context

When you write about context you must make sure that what you write is relevant to the task.

Read this comment by a student about Caroline Bingley:

The letter sent to Jane Bennet by Caroline Bingley inviting her to Netherfield to dine with her and her sister expresses the potential boredom and emptiness of the lives of well-to-do young women who are not married and have no work. The Bingley sisters have many social advantages such as good education and a comfortable house but they do not have the freedom of action of the male members of the family. Caroline's only aim in life is to get Mr Darcy to marry her.

❶ Why is this an effective paragraph about context? Select a), b) or c).

   a) Because it explains how boring Caroline Bingley is.

   b) Because it makes the link between Caroline Bingley's social situation and her character.

   c) Because it tells us what young leisured women did in the early nineteenth century.

EXPLAINING – YOUR TURN!

❷ Now read the following paragraph, and complete it by choosing a suitable point related to context, selecting from a), b) or c) below.

Marriage is presented as the only respectable way for young women of the middle and upper classes to achieve independence from their birth families and gain homes of their own. Young unmarried men are therefore automatically desirable and of the five such at the beginning of the novel only one, Colonel Fitzwilliam, is still single at the end. Charlotte Lucas's comments reveal her private desperation for a home of her own. She considers ...

   a) *that Mr Darcy is a 'very fine young man, with family, fortune, every thing in his favour'.*

   b) *that Jane 'should make the most of every half hour in which she can command his [Bingley's] attention'.*

   c) *that Mr Collins is 'neither sensible nor agreeable [...] but still he [will] be her husband'.*

❸ Now, starting here and continuing onto a sheet of paper, write a paragraph about how Austen uses the context of a small-scale county neighbourhood to show the limitations of everyday existence for young women and the excitement created by the arrival of new people, especially potential husbands.

Austen shows how ... .

....

....

....

....

....

....

PROGRESS LOG [tick the correct box]   Needs more work ☐   Getting there ☐   Under control ☐

Structure and linking of paragraphs

Paragraphs need to demonstrate your points clearly by:

- using topic sentences
- focusing on key words from quotations
- explaining their effect or meaning

① Read this model paragraph in which a student explains how Jane Austen presents Mr Collins:

Even before Mr Collins arrives, Austen makes it clear that he is both ignorant and conceited. 'Can he be a sensible man, sir?' Elizabeth asks her father as soon as she has listened to Mr Collins's letter. Her word 'sensible' means rational but also self-aware or sensitive. Mr Collins is none of those things.

Look at the response carefully.

- **Underline** the topic sentence which explains the main point about Mr Collins.
- **Circle** the word that is picked out from the quotation.
- **Highlight** or put a tick next to the part of the last sentence which explains the word.

② Now read this paragraph by a student who is explaining how Jane Austen presents Mr Bingley:

We first encounter Mr Bingley at the Meryton Assembly. Later he is reported as saying that he had 'never met with pleasanter people or prettier girls in his life'. This shows what a good person he is.

> **Expert viewpoint:** This paragraph is unclear. It does not begin with a topic sentence to explain how Austen presents Mr Bingley and doesn't zoom in on any key words that tell us what Bingley is like.

Now **rewrite the paragraph**. Start with a **topic sentence**, and pick out a **key word or phrase** to 'zoom in' on, then follow up with an explanation or interpretation.

Jane Austen presents Mr Bingley as ... .

....

....

....

....

....

....

....

....

| PROGRESS LOG [tick the correct box] | Needs more work ☐ | Getting there ☐ | Under control ☐ |

It is equally important to make your sentences link together and your ideas follow on fluently from each other. You can do this by:

- using a mixture of short and long sentences as appropriate
- using words or phrases that help connect or develop ideas

❸ Read this model paragraph by one student writing about Kitty Bennet and how she is presented:

Although Kitty Bennet is not one of the novel's main characters, Austen presents her as someone who is influenced by other people and by her environment and who may therefore be capable of change. Kitty is regularly described as 'fretful'. This suggests that she is not happy with her life. It's a measure of Mr and Mrs Bennet's failure as parents that it is Jane and Elizabeth who finally enable Kitty to develop when they have better homes than Longbourn in which to nurture her.

Look at the response carefully.

- **Underline** the topic sentence which introduces the main idea.
- **Underline** the short sentence which signals a change in ideas.
- **Circle** any words or phrases that link ideas such as 'who', 'when', 'implying', 'which', etc.

❹ Read this paragraph by another student commenting on how Lydia Bennet is presented:

Austen gives us a vivid picture of Lydia Bennet. She is the youngest of the sisters and her mother's favourite. She is introduced as 'the tallest' and she speaks 'stoutly'. Lydia is often seen behaving actively. She is almost entirely interested in herself. She also likes clothes, games and flirting. She does not mature.

Expert viewpoint: The candidate has understood how the character's nature is revealed in her appearance and actions. However, the paragraph is rather awkwardly written. It needs improving by linking the sentences with suitable phrases and joining words such as: 'but', 'yet', 'where', 'in', 'as well as', 'who', 'suggesting', 'implying'.

Rewrite the **paragraph**, improving the style, and also try to add a **concluding sentence** summing up Austen's presentation of Lydia as a 'flat' character (incapable of change).

Start with the same **topic sentence**, but extend it:

Austen gives us a vivid picture of Lydia Bennet ... .

....

....

....

....

....

....

....

....

....

PROGRESS LOG [tick the correct box]   Needs more work ☐   Getting there ☐   Under control ☐

Writing skills

Here are a number of key words you might use when writing in the exam:

Content and structure	Characters and style	Linguistic features
chapter	character	rhetoric
scene	role	voice
quotation	protagonist	juxtaposition
sequence	dramatic	dramatic irony
dialogue	caricature	repetition
climax	satirical	omniscient
development	humorous	foreshadowing
description	sympathetic	euphemism

❶ Circle any you might find difficult to spell, and then use the 'Look, Say, Cover, Write, Check' method to learn them. This means: **look** at the word; **say** it out loud; then **cover** it up; **write** it out; uncover and **check** your spelling with the correct version.

❷ Create a **mnemonic** for five of your difficult spellings. For example:

Omniscient: **o**h **m**y **n**ew **i**mage **s**oon **c**ollapsed **i**nto **e**mbarrassment '**n**' **t**ears

Or break the word down: OM – NIS – CI – ENT

a) ....

b) ....

c) ....

d) ....

e) ....

❸ Circle any **incorrect spellings** in this paragraph and then rewrite it correctly:

Austen has already depicked Lady Catherine as a caracture who is used to having her own way. Only Elizabeth's quickness with dialog enables her to cope with Lady Catherine's verbal bullying when she calls at Longborne. Finally however, after the retorickle question 'Are the shades of Pembly to be this polluted?' Elizabeth resorts to neggativity and silence – thus demonstring her capacity for self-restraint.

....

....

....

....

....

....

*AO4 is assessed by OCR only.

❹ **Punctuation** can help make your meaning clear.

Here is one response by a student commenting on Meryton as a centre for social life. Check for correct use of:

- apostrophes
- speech marks for quotations and emphasis
- full stops, commas and capital letters

Meryton is the place where people go to have fun such as attending an assembly or going shopping or visiting aunt philips for a gossip as the country life is so mundane for the girls it isnt surprising that theyre glad when the regiment arrives after they've left for brighton it's a month before kitty can enter meryton without tears notices elizabeth

Rewrite it **correctly** here:

....
....
....
....
....
....

❺ It is better to use the **present tense** to describe what is happening in the novel. Look at these two extracts. Which one uses tenses **consistently** and **accurately**?

Student A: *Austen uses Mr and Mrs Gardiner as a counterbalance to Mr and Mrs Bennet. Although Mr Gardiner was Mrs Bennet's brother he was a very different character. He was intelligent and 'gentlemanlike' despite his office in Cheapside. In the crisis he is calm, effective and communicated regularly with his wife.*

Student B: *Austen uses Mr and Mrs Gardiner as a counterbalance to Mr and Mrs Bennet. Although Mr Gardiner is Mrs Bennet's brother he is a very different character. He is intelligent and 'gentlemanlike' despite his office in Cheapside. In the crisis he is calm, effective and communicates regularly with his wife.*

❻ Now look at this further paragraph. Underline or circle all the **verbs** first.

It was fortunate that Mrs Bennet and Lydia were unaware that Elizabeth was pleading with Mr Bennet to forbid Lydia to go to Brighton. Elizabeth is afraid that Lydia would become 'the most determined flirt' whilst Lydia was already dreaming of 'tenderly flirting with at least six officers at once'.

Now rewrite it using the **present tense** consistently:

....
....
....
....
....
....

PROGRESS LOG [tick the correct box]   Needs more work ☐   Getting there ☐   Under control ☐

Tackling exam tasks (A01) (A02)

DECODING QUESTIONS

It is important to be able to identify key words in exam tasks and then quickly generate some ideas.

❶ Read this task and notice how the key words have been underlined.

Question: *In what ways* does *Elizabeth* *relate to* her *mother* *throughout* the novel?

Write about:

- Elizabeth's behaviour with, and response to, her mother
- The methods Austen uses to present these interactions

Now do the same with this task, i.e. underline the key words:

Question: *How does Austen present the links between social class, money and manners?*

Write about:

- The different social position, wealth and behaviour of characters
- The methods Austen uses to highlight these links

GENERATING IDEAS

❷ Now you need to generate ideas quickly. Use the spider diagram* below and add as many ideas of your own as you can:

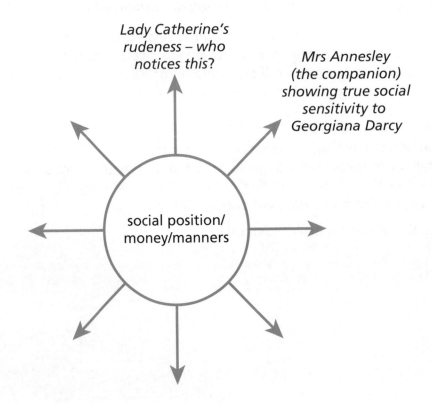

Lady Catherine's rudeness – who notices this?

Mrs Annesley (the companion) showing true social sensitivity to Georgiana Darcy

social position/money/manners

*You could do this as a list if you wish.

PLANNING AN ESSAY

Here is the **exam-style** task from the previous page:

Question: *How does Austen present the links between social class, money and manners?*

Write about:

- The different social position, wealth and behaviour of characters
- The methods Austen uses to highlight these links

❸ **Using the ideas you generated,** write a simple plan with at least **five key points** (the first two have been provided for you). Check back to your spider diagram or the list you made.

a) *Austen makes us aware of nuances of class difference such as whether wealth has come from property or trade.*

b) *Darcy is the richest person and has highest status but initially his manners are found wanting.*

c) ....

....

d) ....

....

e) ....

....

❹ Now list **five quotations,** one for each point (the first two have been provided for you):

a) *Narrator (re Bingley sisters): 'their brother's fortune and their own had been acquired by trade'*

b) *Narrator (re Darcy): 'he was discovered to be proud [...] and not all his large establishment in Derbyshire could then save him'*

c) ....

....

d) ....

....

e) ....

....

❺ Now read this task and **write a plan of your own,** including **quotations,** on a separate sheet of paper.

Read from *'Colonel Fitzwilliam's manners were very much admired at the parsonage'* to *'and made no answer'* (Vol. 2, Ch. 8, pp. 142–4).

Question: *How does Austen use the interplay between characters to explore the theme of manners? Comment on the extract and the novel as a whole.*

PROGRESS LOG [tick the correct box]   Needs more work ☐   Getting there ☐   Under control ☐

Sample answers

OPENING PARAGRAPHS

Read this task:

Question: *How does Jane Austen depict the relationship between gentry (middle and upper classes) and servants?*

Now look at these two alternative openings to the essay and read the examiner comments underneath:

Student A

> *'Pride and Prejudice' has a very narrow social world. When you read it you can see that Mr Darcy is much grander than Mr Collins, for instance, and you could begin to assume that that's all there is. When you think about it however you realise that these people are a very small part of the whole range of society – even in Jane Austen's time. Her idea of using the housekeeper to change our views about Mr Darcy is an effective surprise.*

Student B

> *No one seems to notice the people who do the work in 'Pride and Prejudice'. The main characters in the novel sit around getting bored and wondering who to marry and they don't seem to notice anyone else. When Elizabeth actually speaks to a housekeeper it's quite a surprise.*

Expert viewpoint 1: The central idea of this opening paragraph is sound but it is not well expressed. Stylistically this introduction is awkward. A more formal style of writing would have helped convince the reader that the essay would broaden out into a wider discussion and more in-depth analysis of themes.

Expert viewpoint 2: This opening comments on the narrow social world without outlining what is to be discussed in the essay. The student expresses his/her personal disapproval of these limitations without considering Austen's intention.

① Which comment belongs to which answer? Match the paragraph (A or B) to the expert's feedback (1 or 2).

Student A: .... Student B: ....

② Now it's your turn. Write the opening paragraph for this task on a separate sheet of paper:

Read from *'Colonel Fitzwilliam's manners were very much admired at the parsonage'* to *'and made no answer'* (Vol. 2, Ch. 8, pp. 142–4).

Question: *How does Austen use the interplay between characters to explore the theme of manners? Comment on the extract and the novel as a whole.*

Remember:

- Introduce the topic in general terms, perhaps **explaining** or **'unpicking'** the key **words** or **ideas** in the task (such as 'interplay').
- Mention the **different possibilities** or ideas that you are going to address.
- Use the **author's name**.

*AO4 is assessed by OCR only.

WRITING ABOUT TECHNIQUES

Here are two paragraphs in response to a different task, where the students have focused on the writer's techniques. The task is:

Read from *'If Elizabeth, when Mr Darcy gave her the letter'* to *'entirely blameless throughout the whole'* (Vol. 2, Ch. 13, pp. 169–70).

Question: *What techniques does Austen use to show the impact of Darcy's letter on Elizabeth?*

Student A

> Austen says Elizabeth is prejudiced 'with a strong prejudice against everything he might say'. She doesn't like his style of writing. Austen shows Elizabeth reading as she walks and then putting the letter away and taking it out again and rereading. She can't help realising that facts as told by Darcy are not the same as those she heard from Wickham. Who is right?

Student B

> Elizabeth's mental confusion and gradual understanding of the situation are made vivid by Austen's description of her reported reception of Darcy's letter. She begins 'with a strong prejudice against everything he might say'. This links the scene at once to the novel's title and the link is reinforced as Elizabeth condemns Darcy's style as being 'all pride and insolence'. Austen brings the reader close to Elizabeth's physical existence as she puts the letter 'hastily' away and almost immediately it 'was unfolded again'. Elizabeth is intelligent, rational and has a sense of justice. Soon she begins to analyse what is written and begins to accept the truth.

Expert viewpoint 1: This response describes the impact of Darcy's words on Elizabeth. It also states the link between this scene and the wider themes of prejudice and pride and offers appropriate evidence. It discusses the writer's techniques, using literary terms (such as 'reception') to good effect.

High level

Expert viewpoint 2: This response describes the impact of Darcy's words on Elizabeth. However, the quotation, though appropriate, is not fluently embedded in the sentence. There is one instance of the writer's technique mentioned but no others and in the final sentence the point made is not developed and no evidence or examples are given.

Mid level

❸ Which comment belongs to which answer? Match the paragraph (A or B) to the expert's feedback (1 or 2).

Student A: .... Student B: ....

❹ Now, take another **aspect** of the scene and on a separate sheet of paper write your own paragraph. You could **comment** on one of these aspects:

- The process of reading
- Elizabeth's inner monologue
- The change in Austen's writing style as Elizabeth becomes calmer

PART SIX: Progress Booster

Now read this **lower-level** response to the following task:

Read from *'Colonel Fitzwilliam's manners were very much admired at the parsonage'* to *'and made no answer'* (Vol. 2, Ch. 8, pp. 142–4).

Question: *How does Austen use the interplay between characters to explore the theme of manners? Comment on the extract and the novel as a whole.*

Student response

> The narrator tells us that Colonel Fitzwilliam is attracted to Elizabeth. 'Mrs Collins's pretty friend.' His good manners are contrasted with Lady Catherine's arrogance. He and Darcy are bored as they pay their visit to their aunt. Also Lady Catherine has rudely neglected to invite the Collinses and their guests until now as she has posher guests. She can't bear it when Colonel Fitzwilliam is talking to Elizabeth and not to her.
>
> There's a lot of comedy in the way that Lady Catherine says she likes music but hasn't ever bothered to learn. She says her own daughter is too sickly and sends lots of bossy instructions to Darcy's sister Georgiana which don't sound as if they are needed.

Expert viewpoint: The quotation in the first paragraph is well chosen and gives us a sense of Elizabeth's natural attractiveness, but there is no an attempt to embed it in a sentence. Nor is there sufficient exploration of the interplay between characters as instructed by the question. Comments on what Austen intends in this scene are needed, and the language the student uses is sometimes too informal, as in 'posher guests'.

⑤ Rewrite these two **paragraphs** in your own words, improving them by addressing:

- The lack of development of linking of points – no **'zooming in'** on **key words and phrases**
- The lack of **quotations and embedding**
- Unnecessary **repetition**, poor **specialist terms** and use of **vocabulary**

Paragraph 1: *In this scene, Austen uses the easy intelligent conversation between Elizabeth and Colonel Fitzwilliam to* ....

....

and contrasts it with ....

This highlights the ....

....

....

....

Paragraph 2: *Austen's comic presentation of Lady Catherine's feeling of exclusion is* ....

....

Mr Darcy's involvement is expressed as ....

This links to the novel's preoccupation with ....

....

....

A FULL-LENGTH RESPONSE

⑥ Write a full-length response to this exam-style task on a separate sheet of paper. Answer both parts of the question:

Question: *Explore the importance of Lady Catherine de Bourgh both to the action of the novel and to its overall style and themes.*

Write about:

- Lady Catherine's importance to the plot
- How Lady Catherine's character contributes to the themes

Remember to do the following:

- Plan **quickly** (no more than 5 minutes) what you intend to write, jotting down **four or five supporting quotations**.
- Refer closely to the **key words** in the question.
- Make sure you comment on **what** the writer does, the **techniques** she uses and the **effect** of those techniques.
- Support your points with **well-chosen quotations** or other evidence.
- Develop your points by '**zooming in**' on particular **words** or **phrases** and explaining their **effect**.
- Be **persuasive** and **convincing** in what you say.
- Check carefully for **spelling**, **punctuation** and **grammar**.

PROGRESS LOG [tick the correct box]   Needs more work ☐   Getting there ☐   Under control ☐

Further questions

❶ Do you think Elizabeth and Darcy are likely to be happy? What evidence do you have for your view?

❷ Lydia's elopement provokes a crisis in the Bennet family. Do you think Mr and Mrs Bennet will be permanently changed by it?

❸ Comment on Jane Austen's use of the narrator.

❹ Relate the beginning of the novel to its happy ending.

❺ To what extent does *Pride and Prejudice* reflect its title?

PROGRESS LOG [tick the correct box]   Needs more work ☐   Getting there ☐   Under control ☐

ANSWERS

NOTE: Answers have been provided for most tasks. Exceptions are 'Practice tasks' and tasks which ask you to write a paragraph or use your own words or judgement.

PART TWO: PLOT AND ACTION [pp. 8–44]

Volume 1, Chapters 1–2 [pp. 8–9]

1 a) T; b) F; c) T; d) F; e) T; f) F; g) T

2 a) An unmarried man who has money is immediately interesting and attractive to any family with unmarried daughters.

b) None of them is married. Jane is 'handsome', Lizzy is quick, Mary reads 'great books', Kitty coughs and Lydia speaks 'stoutly'.

c) They are all interested in a young man with money and are eager to get to know him. They gossip about each other and sound competitive.

3

Point/detail	Evidence	Effect or explanation
1: Mr Bennet seems to know exactly how to annoy Mrs Bennet.	Mr Bennet: 'I must throw in a good word for my little Lizzy.' Mrs Bennet: 'I desire you will do no such thing.'	Mrs Bennet's irritation is immediate and their exchange marks Elizabeth out from the other daughters. Mr Bennet favours her but Mrs Bennet does not.
2: Austen shows Mr Bennet to be weary of his marriage and his wife's hypochondria (her nerves).	He says he has heard her talk about her nerves 'these twenty years at least'.	Although Mr Bennet claims to 'respect' Mrs Bennet's nerves, his tone is not sympathetic and she seems aware of this: 'you do not know what I suffer'.
3: The narrator's comments at the end leave no doubt about Mrs Bennet's failings.	'She was a woman of mean understanding, little information and uncertain temper.'	The narrator's lack of sympathy with Mrs Bennet is emphasised by the strong rhetorical rhythm of the sentences, e.g. this build-up of three clauses.

Volume 1, Chapters 3–6 [pp. 10–11]

1 a) wealth; b) tolerable; c) Bingley's admiration for Darcy's judgement; d) show her feelings; e) playfulness

2 a) Bingley admires Jane and thinks she is beautiful. She is falling in love with him but is too uncertain to show her feelings.

b) The Bingley sisters are good looking and smartly dressed. They can be pleasant when it suits them but are also snobbish and 'conceited' (p. 11).

c) The guests at the assembly see Darcy's pride as arrogance and conceit. Charlotte Lucas thinks pride is a version of self-esteem.

3

Point/detail	Evidence	Effect or explanation
1: Charlotte thinks Jane should make every effort to get Bingley to propose.	'She may lose the opportunity of fixing him'.	Charlotte's language suggests she has a strategic approach to finding a husband.
2: Elizabeth says that Jane needs to be sure of her feelings and needs time to get to know Bingley.	'She has known him only a fortnight.'	Charlotte and Elizabeth agree that Jane has never been alone with Bingley. Charlotte doesn't think this matters; Elizabeth does.
3: Austen shows that Elizabeth is unaware of the extent of the difference between herself and Charlotte.	'You would never act in this way yourself.'	This is an example of narrative irony as it's exactly how Charlotte acts. It also shows Elizabeth as naïve.

Volume 1, Chapters 7–8 [pp. 12–13]

1 Winter in the countryside could be very dull for unmarried women of the higher social **class**, who were not expected to work. Lydia and Kitty Bennet's lives are changed by the arrival of a Militia **regiment** in the nearby town of **Meryton** where their aunt and uncle live. They walk there every day to gossip about the **officers**. The Bingley sisters are also bored and invite Jane to **dine** with them. Mrs Bennet schemes for Jane to be caught in the rain so that she will have to stay for the **night**. Jane falls ill and Elizabeth walks across **fields** to be with her. The Bingley sisters are shocked by Elizabeth's **appearance**.

2 a) Mr Bennet thinks that Kitty and Lydia are 'two of the silliest girls in the country' (p. 22). Mrs Bennet is much more sympathetic.

b) Mrs Bennet tells Mr Bennet not to let Jane have the carriage so that she has to ride and will get caught in the rain.

c) She should be able to sing, to play, to draw, to dance, to do needlework, to speak foreign languages, to read widely and to 'possess a certain something' (p. 31).

3

Point/detail	Evidence	Effect or explanation
1: Mary Bennet is critical of Elizabeth and expresses herself pompously.	'Exertion should always be in proportion to what is required'.	Mary's statement sounds impressive but her abstract words reveal no true concern for Jane's illness.
2: Austen selects active words and an energetic rhythm to describe Elizabeth's walk.	'crossing', 'jumping,' 'springing', 'glowing'	These active words give a warm, positive effect which contrasts with the negative comments of the Bingley sisters.
3: Mr Hurst's lack of reaction contrasts with Mr Darcy's complex response.	Mr Hurst thinks 'only of his breakfast'.	Mr Hurst's reaction is an example of Austen using a concrete detail to reveal small-mindedness. Mr Darcy is described as 'divided'.

Volume 1, Chapters 9–12 [pp. 14–15]

1 a) Charlotte Lucas; b) Mr Darcy; c) Elizabeth; d) Jane; e) Mr Bingley; f) Miss Bingley and Mrs Hurst (Bingley sisters); g) Miss Darcy

2 a) Mrs Bennet thinks she has won an argument when she says she dines with twenty-four families. She has no idea that she is being ridiculous when she thinks a neighbourhood is as big as a city.

b) She agrees with everything he says. She flatters his sister and is ready to criticise her own brother.

c) Mr Bennet is glad to see them as the family evening conversation has been dull without them. Mrs Bennet thinks they should have stayed longer.

3

Point/detail	Evidence	Effect or explanation
1: Bingley's overhasty decisions and his deference to Darcy are discussed at length.	Elizabeth: 'To yield readily – easily – to the persuasion of a friend is no merit with you.'	This is ironic. Elizabeth thinks she is defending Bingley's kind nature when in fact his weakness of character will hurt Jane.
2: Bingley leaving Netherfield is mentioned as a specific possibility.	'I should probably be off in five minutes'.	An example of narrative irony. Bingley is only saying this to make a point but later he leaves hastily for London.
3: Austen shows Elizabeth trying to defend Bingley then realising that Darcy's feelings have been hurt.	Elizabeth 'thought she could perceive that he was rather offended; and therefore checked her laugh.'	Although Elizabeth is sensitive to both men's feelings she doesn't see far enough below the surface to understand how strongly Bingley is dominated by Darcy.

Volume 1, Chapters 13–17 [pp. 16–17]

1 a) F; b) F; c) T; d) F; e) F; f) F; g) T

2 a) She is his patron, which means that he relies on her for his position as a clergyman. She is very rich and grand but has been kind to him.

b) Wickham is good looking, charming and easy to talk to. He has good manners and is about to join the Militia, which will mean he will be wearing officer uniform and have some authority.

c) Mr Bennet thinks Mr Collins is pompous and not a 'sensible man'. He encourages him to reveal his stupidity but after a while he wants to retreat to his library to escape from his guest.

3

Point/detail	Evidence	Effect or explanation
1: Mrs Bennet is described as 'beyond the reach of reason' on the subject of the entail yet today's readers may agree with much of what she says.	'If I had been you, I should have tried long ago to do something or other about it.'	At this point in the novel the reader's sympathy is with Mr Bennet. Later it becomes obvious that he has been lazy in not saving for his daughters' future.
2: Mr Bennet is neither thoughtful nor sensitive in the way he announces Mr Collins's visit.	He says Mr Collins 'may turn you all out of this house'.	The narrator describes Mr Bennet as 'amusing himself' with his announcement. There is no comment on this selfishness.

| 3: Mr Collins reserves the power to reveal his plans at a moment to suit him. | 'but of this hereafter' | He hasn't met his cousins when he writes this letter and his constant focus on himself reveals that he is totally self-centred. |

Volume 1, Chapters 18–21 [pp. 18–19]

1 a) Mr Wickham; b) Mr Bennet; c) is following female convention; d) his pride is hurt; e) wants her brother to marry Miss Darcy

2 a) Darcy's expression changes but he doesn't say anything for a moment. When he does speak it is obvious he's struggling to be polite as well as honest.

b) Mrs Bennet talks loudly and constantly about her expectation that Bingley and Jane will soon be married. She is also rude about Mr Darcy although she knows he can hear her.

c) Mr Bennet's library is the place where he goes to escape his family. It's traditionally a male space and he dislikes being forced to share it with Mr Collins.

3

Point/detail	Evidence	Effect or explanation
1: Mr Collins tells Elizabeth that no one else will want to marry her as she has so little money.	'Your portion is unhappily so small that it will in all likelihood undo the effects of your loveliness'.	Not only is this unromantic and insulting, it also highlights how little power women with no money of their own had over their futures.
2: In contrast to Mr Collins's pomposity, Elizabeth's speech is balanced, intelligent and clear.	Elizabeth asks, 'Can I speak plainer?'	This is a rhetorical question as the reader can see (though Mr Collins cannot) that she makes herself completely clear.
3: Elizabeth decides she must ask her father for help if Mr Collins will not listen to her.	She thinks at least her father's behaviour 'could not be mistaken for the affectation [...] of an elegant female.'	Elizabeth's thought is both comic and a bitter reflection of her own ultimate powerlessness.

Volume 1, Chapters 22–3 [pp. 20–1]

1 The Lucas family are **delighted** when Mr Collins asks their permission to marry Charlotte. She is already **twenty-seven** years old and is neither pretty nor rich. Marriage to Mr Collins will give her her own **home** and then, when Mr Bennet dies, she will be able to move into **Longbourn**. Charlotte's marriage will make it easier for her younger **sisters** to attend social occasions and try to attract husbands for themselves. It also means that her **brothers** won't need to support her when their father dies. Charlotte herself is prepared to overlook all Mr Collins's shortcomings for the sake of **marriage**. She is only worried about losing **Elizabeth's** friendship.

2 a) Elizabeth has never fully understood that Charlotte meant what she said about marrying for money. She is surprised by the speed of Charlotte's decision.

b) Charlotte says she is not a romantic and only wants a comfortable home. She believes happiness in marriage is entirely a matter of chance.

ANSWERS

c) At first Elizabeth exclaims that this is 'impossible!' She quickly realises that this is not polite and manages to control herself and offer Charlotte her congratulations.

3

Point/detail	Evidence	Effect or explanation
1: In Chapter 1, Mrs Bennet announced Bingley's arrival and raised hopes of marriage. She is distraught now he has left.	Initially, Mrs Bennet said: 'What a fine thing for our girls!' Now she is 'really in a most pitiable state'.	The focus on Mrs Bennet keeps the tone satirical. Austen highlights her inconsistency and self-delusion instead of focusing directly on Jane's heartbreak.
2: The balance of power between Mrs Bennet and Lady Lucas has shifted.	In Chapter 1 the Lucases were quick to visit Netherfield in pursuit of an unmarried man. Now Lady Lucas visits Longbourn and feels 'triumph'.	Success or failure in the marriage market affects the relationship between the Bennets and their neighbours throughout the novel. This unspoken competitiveness is part of the satire of society.
3: Mrs Bennet's selfishness makes Jane's situation even more painful.	Jane needs all her 'steady mildness' to cope with Mrs Bennet's complaints about Bingley's absence.	Austen's choice of words expresses what Jane can't say aloud. Mrs Bennet lacks 'delicacy'. She 'attacks' and Jane can only manage 'tolerable tranquillity'.

Volume 2, Chapters 1–3 [pp. 22–3]

1 a) Mr Bingley; b) Charlotte Lucas; c) Mr Collins; d) Mr Wickham; e) Mr Gardiner; f) Mrs Gardiner; g) Miss Bingley

2 a) Elizabeth thinks Jane is 'too good' because she won't say or think anything negative about Bingley leaving. Jane is struggling to convince herself that she has simply made a mistake.

b) Mrs Bennet complains that she could have had two daughters married but now has none. She blames Elizabeth for refusing Mr Collins and is angry that Lady Lucas will have a daughter married before her.

c) Elizabeth notices how careful Charlotte is to write positively about her new home and Lady Catherine.

3

Point/detail	Evidence	Effect or explanation
1: Unlike Elizabeth, Jane had continued to trust Miss Bingley's friendship even after Mr Bingley had rejected her.	'I confess myself to have been entirely deceived'.	'Confess' and 'entirely deceived' are strong words. Jane is kind but not stupid. Once the evidence is clear she does not hesitate to admit her mistakes.
2: Jane judges Miss Bingley on her failure to write or return calls and on her behaviour when she visits.	'When she did come it was very evident she had no pleasure in it.'	Miss Bingley's rudeness is expressed through her negativity. 'She had no pleasure'. She said 'not a word'.

3: This letter gives insight into Jane's mind as she struggles to understand how she has misread the situation.	'considering what her behaviour was, my confidence was as natural as your suspicion'	The language gives the impression that Jane is using the letter to talk directly to Elizabeth. As well as describing present feelings she thinks back to the past.

Volume 2, Chapters 4–5 [pp. 24–5]

1 a) T; b) F; c) F; d) T; e) F; f) T; g) T

2 a) Mrs Gardiner is especially fond of Jane and Elizabeth and is sensitive to their feelings. She takes a more responsible attitude than their parents do and is prepared to give them good advice.

b) Elizabeth admires Charlotte's strategies for keeping Mr Collins out of her way. She also notices that Charlotte is enjoying making her house comfortable and is tactful even when her husband says something embarrassing or shows his 'stupidity'.

c) When Miss de Bourgh pauses outside the parsonage Charlotte and Mr Collins stand outside talking to her while Sir William Lucas bows from the doorway. Maria Lucas rushes upstairs to Elizabeth 'breathless with agitation' (p. 132).

3

Point/detail	Evidence	Effect or explanation
1: Mr Collins is as pompous and conceited in his own home as he is elsewhere. Marriage has not changed this.	'Elizabeth was prepared to see him in his glory'.	Mr Collins enjoys showing off his home and surroundings. He wants Elizabeth to recognise all that she has missed.
2: Austen suggests that Charlotte controls her true feelings.	Elizabeth 'admired the command of countenance with which Charlotte talked'.	Austen makes use of body language to show the extent of Charlotte's self-control. Only occasionally does Elizabeth discern 'a faint blush'.
3: Charlotte finds pleasure in her housekeeping when Mr Collins is not around.	'When Mr Collins could be forgotten, there was really a great air of comfort throughout'.	Either Elizabeth or the narrator is always ready with a sarcastic reminder. In this case Elizabeth 'supposed he must be often forgotten'.

Volume 2, Chapters 6–10 [pp. 26–7]

1 a) overpowered; b) intrusive; c) call at Hunsford Parsonage; d) music; e) sits in silence

2 a) Elizabeth sees that Rosings is a fine house in an attractive park but she cannot summon as much enthusiasm as Mr Collins expects.

b) He leaves his place next to Lady Catherine and comes to stand close to Elizabeth where he can watch and listen and then enjoy a friendly, teasing conversation with her.

c) Colonel Fitzwilliam explains that although he is the younger son of an earl he cannot please himself when he chooses a wife. He must marry someone with money. Elizabeth wonders if he is dropping her a hint.

3

Point/detail	Evidence	Effect or explanation
1: When Lady Catherine visits Hunsford she assumes the authority to interfere in the minutest details of daily life.	'She examined [...] their work, and advised them to do it differently.'	We can see the use of the word 'advised' as ironic as Lady Catherine has very strong views and expects to be obeyed.
2: Lady Catherine is economically powerful.	'Elizabeth recollected that there might be other family livings to be disposed of'.	Lady Catherine has the power to appoint clergymen, like Mr Collins, to 'livings' (paid jobs in different parishes) and so Elizabeth realises that Charlotte is being strategic.
3: There is little to do at the Parsonage (except visit Rosings) but Elizabeth escapes Lady Catherine's company when she can.	'where she felt beyond the reach of Lady Catherine's curiosity'	The world of young leisured women in the novel is one where it is difficult to be alone – especially in the orbit of Rosings Park.

Volume 2, Chapter 11 [pp. 28–9]

1 The timing of Mr Darcy's **marriage** proposal is especially unfortunate for him. In literary terms it is an example of narrative **irony**. Elizabeth has just been told by **Colonel Fitzwilliam** of the part Darcy played in preventing Bingley's **marriage** to Jane. She is extremely upset by this so has stayed behind in the parsonage while the others have gone to dine at **Rosings**. To make matters worse she has been rereading all the **letters** that Jane has sent her since she has been away. Elizabeth can see Jane is not **happy** and therefore becomes even more distressed herself. She hears the door bell and a few moments later **Darcy** walks into the room.

2 a) When Darcy enters the room he is agitated and cannot sit or stand still. However once he has made his proposal he looks calm and confident and leans against the mantelpiece watching Elizabeth.

b) Initially Elizabeth is amazed. She realises this is a real compliment.

c) Elizabeth has never wanted Darcy to like her. He is the person who has ruined Jane's happiness and she also blames him for his behaviour to Wickham.

3

Point/detail	Evidence	Effect or explanation
1: Darcy's immediate reaction is to accuse Elizabeth of rudeness.	He asks: 'Why, with so little endeavour at civility, I am thus rejected'?	The reader will by now have noticed that Darcy always retreats into arrogance when he is upset. He speaks stiffly and this begins to anger Elizabeth.
2: Elizabeth's pride is also hurt and she accuses Darcy of rudeness in the language of his proposal.	He has told her that he likes her 'against [his] will.'	Although Darcy does not react here we discover later that it is her criticisms of his ungentlemanlike behaviour that have hurt him the most.

3: Darcy finally responds by telling Elizabeth exactly what he thinks of her family.	He describes 'the inferiority of her connections'.	This pompous criticism of Elizabeth's 'inferior' family hurts her deeply.

Volume 2, Chapters 12–13 [pp. 30–1]

1 a) Mr Darcy; b) Jane Bennet; c) Mr Wickham; d) Georgiana Darcy; e) Mr Wickham

2 a) The letter begins with a stiff and offended tone. When Darcy talks about Jane he admits he may have been wrong; he apologises for his remarks on Elizabeth's family, defends himself reasonably concerning Mr Wickham and ends kindly, saying 'God bless you' (p. 168).

b) He noticed that Bingley's feelings for Jane were serious and realised people expected them to marry. He also saw more bad behaviour by members of the Bennet family.

c) Parts of the letter make her angry, but as she reads and rereads using her sense of reason and justice, she comes to believe he is right. She is then horrified by her own actions.

3

Point/detail	Evidence	Effect or explanation
1: Elizabeth is using her intellect and sense of fairness to think back and reassess the new evidence concerning Wickham.	'Every lingering struggle in his favour grew fainter and fainter'.	The word 'struggle' reveals Elizabeth's awareness that she wanted to think well of Wickham for emotional reasons but now she cannot.
2: The long first paragraph of this extract is expressed in formal language, almost like a summing up.	The choice of language includes words such as 'proved', 'motive', 'questioned.'	These words give an impression of an enquiry. They are used by the narrator, which gives them seriousness, but they are also Elizabeth's own conclusions.
3: The style of writing shifts to express Elizabeth's emotional response.	'How despicably have I acted!' she cried.	The sudden change to direct speech and an exclamatory style shows how the realisation of her mistakes affects Elizabeth emotionally.

Volume 2, Chapters 14–19 [pp. 32–3]

1 a) F; b) T; c) F; d) T; e) F; f) T

2 a) Lydia and Kitty come to meet their sisters and order lunch at the inn. However Lydia has to borrow the money for lunch as she has spent hers on a bonnet. She tells stories about the officers all the way home.

b) Jane finds it hard to believe that anyone could behave so badly but agrees with Elizabeth that they are not obliged to tell everyone the truth, as Wickham will soon be leaving the neighbourhood and there is so much prejudice against Darcy that they would probably not be believed.

c) Elizabeth is disappointed that they won't have time to reach the Lakes and is a little apprehensive at the prospect of entering Derbyshire, Mr Darcy's county. However she knows she is going to enjoy travelling with her uncle and aunt.

ANSWERS

3

Point/detail	Evidence	Effect or explanation
1: Lydia's behaviour is typically self-centred, insensitive and physically wild.	'Wholly inattentive to her sister's feelings, Lydia flew about the house'.	The narrator's observation that Lydia is 'wholly inattentive' emphasises her lack of sympathy for Kitty. The strong verbs (e.g. 'flew') express her uncontrolled energy.
2: Elizabeth is aware of the way Lydia's inappropriate behaviour affects the whole family.	'[She] will, at sixteen, be the most determined flirt that ever made herself and her family ridiculous'.	Elizabeth's strong and sincere speech contrasts with her father's flippant 'What, has she frightened away some of your lovers? Poor little Lizzy!'
3: Mr Bennet's response shows his affection for Elizabeth but also his laziness.	'We shall have no peace at Longbourn if Lydia does not go to Brighton'.	Mr Bennet avoids difficulties by doing nothing – his main aim is to have a peaceful house.

Volume 3, Chapters 1–3 [pp. 34–5]

1 a) approachable and generous to the poor; b) by accident; c) extremely shy; d) tanned complexion; e) Mr Darcy

2 a) Elizabeth first sees Pemberley as it opens out before her in a spectacular natural setting. The pleasant company of her uncle and aunt allow her to enjoy it fully rather than having everything explained by Mr Collins. Rosings shows riches: Pemberley expresses good taste.

b) Mr Darcy brings his sister Georgiana to meet Elizabeth immediately she arrives at Pemberley. This is much sooner than politeness demands and Mr and Mrs Gardiner begin to wonder whether Mr Darcy is attracted to their niece.

c) Georgiana's shyness and fear of doing the wrong thing make her behave awkwardly in company.

3

Point/detail	Evidence	Effect or explanation
1: Elizabeth Darcy expects, to avoid her.	'For a few moments, indeed, she felt he would probably strike into some other path.'	While Elizabeth's speech is hesitant, Darcy shows no hesitation in approaching her.
2: The themes of pride, family, gentlemanliness all come together at this point.	'This was a stroke of civility for which she was quite unprepared.'	The reader is closely in tune with Elizabeth's thoughts and feelings as she sees Darcy behaving so politely and knows she can trust her aunt and uncle not to embarrass her.
3: Austen switches from straightforward narration to internal questioning by Elizabeth.	Compare the beginning and end of this section.	At the beginning Elizabeth attempts superficial conversation with Darcy about the beauty of Pemberley: by the end she is silent and asking herself agitated rhetorical questions.

Volume 3, Chapters 4–6 [pp. 36–7]

1 Elizabeth has been expecting **letters** from Jane. Two arrive together and Elizabeth's first clue that all is not well at **Longbourn/home** is Jane's unusually bad handwriting. From then matters grow rapidly worse. The first letter tells the shocking news that Lydia has eloped to **Scotland** with Wickham. Jane is struggling to think **well** of everyone and says this must mean Wickham truly loves Lydia as he knows Mr Bennet won't be able to give her any **money**. The second letter, however, contains the information that Wickham and Lydia are probably in London and are not **married**. Jane begs Elizabeth and the Gardiners to return home as **Mrs Bennet** has collapsed and **Mr Bennet** is angry but ineffective. **Elizabeth** leaps up and runs to the door. At that moment **Mr Darcy** arrives.

2 a) Elizabeth believes she and Darcy will never be able to be happy together again. She thinks back over their relationship and realises how far her feelings for him have changed.

b) Mrs Bennet is most concerned about herself – she thinks Mr Bennet will fight a duel with Wickham and be killed, then she will be turned out by the Collinses.

c) Mr Bennet has gone to London to try to find Wickham and persuade him to marry Lydia. He does not keep in regular touch with the rest of the family and says little when he returns, although he does admit he was wrong not to listen to Elizabeth.

3

Point/detail	Evidence	Effect or explanation
1: Austen uses the arrival or non-arrival of letters to express helplessness and suspense at Longbourn.	'The arrival of letters was the first grand object of every morning's impatience.'	We understand that it is letters from London that are expected by the anxious family. The arrival of a letter from Kent is therefore a surprise.
2: Mr Collins's letter is an unwelcome reminder of the scandal and its lasting damage to all the Bennets.	'For who, as Lady Catherine, so condescendingly observes, will connect themselves with such a family?'	This emphasises the importance of reputation and also the theme of families being involved in each other's behaviour.
3: Mr Collins pretends he is writing to sympathise but his letter is entirely negative and uncharitable.	'The death of your daughter would have been a blessing in comparison'.	This letter could have provided comic relief but it is a harsh, satirical form of humour. Mr Collins is a clergyman but his letter contains no compassion or forgiveness.

Volume 3, Chapters 7–10 [pp. 38–9]

1 a) Mr Wickham; b) Mr Bennet; c) Mr Darcy; d) Lydia; e) Mr Wickham

2 a) Mrs Gardiner says that Mr Gardiner assumed Darcy wished to act in this way because he had 'another interest in the affair' – i.e. Elizabeth.

b) They imagine she will feel embarrassed and ashamed and grateful – probably rather quiet and shy – just as they would be in her circumstances.

c) Lydia hasn't changed at all. She is noisy and cheerful and keen to show off her ring. She insists that Jane moves lower down the table as she takes precedence now because she's married.

3

Point/detail	Evidence	Effect or explanation
1: Mrs Bennet's reaction to Lydia's elopement has been to withdraw to her room. Now her mood swings to wild excitement.	'I will go to Meryton [...] and tell the good, good news to my sister Philips.'	Mrs Bennet seems to assume that all the shocking circumstances will now be forgotten in the light of this 'good news'.
2: For Mrs Bennet, Lydia's marriage means clothes. She has no awareness of any sacrifice made by anyone else.	'Lizzy, my dear, run down to your father, and ask him how much he will give her.'	Almost all Mrs Bennet's statements are exclamations and she has no time to listen to anyone else or consider alternative points of view. She is a caricature of selfishness.
3: Mrs Bennet sees marriage as an end in itself. She doesn't think about Lydia's future happiness or security.	'She was disturbed by no fear for her felicity'.	As readers we know what Wickham is really like and so Austen's use of the phrase 'no fear' suggests that Mrs Bennet should be feeling the exact opposite.

Volume 3, Chapters 11–15 [pp. 40–1]

1 a) F; b) F; c) T; d) T; e) F; f) F; g) T

2 a) Mrs Bennet is deliberately cold towards Mr Darcy. She talks about Lydia's wedding and states that Mr Wickham does not have as many friends as he deserves, meaning Darcy.

b) Jane is lively, emotional, delighted. She goes to tell her mother the good news without a moment's hesitation.

c) Lady Catherine is stiff and ungracious.

3

Point/detail	Evidence	Effect or explanation
1: Elizabeth's relationship with her father has always been close as they share a sense of humour. On this occasion it is different.	'Never had his wit been directed in a manner so little agreeable to her.'	The emphasis is on 'never'. Austen also shows Elizabeth's struggle to 'force' a 'reluctant' smile. We may wonder why she cannot confide in her father.
2: Mr Bennet is an intelligent man and loves Elizabeth but his view of the world is misguided.	'For what do we live, but to make sport for our neighbours, and laugh at them in our turn?'	Austen is relying on the reader's awareness of Elizabeth's hidden feelings so as to understand that Mr Bennet is wrong, and love is what gives meaning to life.
3: Austen shows us that Elizabeth is suffering from self-doubt. She wonders if her father is right when he speaks of Darcy's lack of interest in her.	'instead of his seeing too little, she might have fancied too much.'	This painful inner turmoil reveals how much Elizabeth has changed from the person who was so sure of herself at the beginning of the novel.

Volume 3, Chapters 16–19 [pp. 42–3]

1 a) loves Elizabeth; b) challenged her prejudices; c) without respect; d) misunderstood her relationship with Darcy; e) astonishment

2 a) Opportunities to talk alone are scarce. Mrs Bennet tries to help Jane and Bingley do so but this is so obvious that it's embarrassing. Walking offers the best option for private conversation.

b) Jane thinks that Elizabeth is joking. Then she wonders whether Elizabeth is making a mistake. Once reassured, she wants to hear all the details.

c) We learn that Lydia doesn't change although her marriage is not a great success. Kitty improves a great deal as she spends most of her time with Jane and Elizabeth: Mary is happy to remain at Longbourn, especially as she no longer suffers comparison with her more beautiful sisters.

3

Point/detail	Evidence	Effect or explanation
1: At the start of the novel people assumed Darcy was proud because of his appearance and lack of conversation. Now he is able to speak for himself.	'I have been a selfish being all my life, in practice, though not in principle.'	For the first time, Austen reveals Darcy's inner thoughts and feelings about his 'life'.
2: Darcy explains that part of his pride has come from a solitary, overprotected childhood.	'I was spoilt by my parents'.	Georgiana, who is much younger than Darcy, also gives the impression that she is proud when she is merely shy and reserved.
3: Darcy is generous in his gratitude to Elizabeth for making him change.	'By you, I was properly humbled.'	He uses emotional language such as 'humbled', 'unworthy' and speaks of his own 'pretensions' and 'vanity'. This shows the strength of his love and convinces the reader that he really has changed.

PART THREE: CHARACTERS [pp. 45–55]

Who's who [p. 45]

1 a) Fitzwilliam Darcy; b) Charles Bingley; c) Lady Catherine de Bourgh; d) George Wickham; e) Mr Bennet; f) Mrs Bennet; g) William Collins; h) Charlotte Lucas; i) Jane Bennet; j) Elizabeth Bennet

Elizabeth Bennet [p. 46]

1 a) F; b) T; c) NEE; d) F; e) F; f) NEE; g) T

2 a) Elizabeth laughs at her friend Charlotte's rational approach to marriage because she can't believe that Charlotte would ever act in such a way herself.

b) In Volume 1, Chapter 11, when Mr Darcy accuses Elizabeth of being too ready to joke about people she defends herself by saying that she only laughs at 'follies and nonsense, whims and inconsistencies'.

c) Elizabeth explains to Colonel Fitzwilliam and Mr Darcy in Volume 2, Chapter 8 that her performance on the piano is not as good as it could be because she doesn't practise often enough.

ANSWERS

d) *When she first hears of the crisis over Lydia's elopement Elizabeth longs to be at home so that she can help Jane bear the burden of their mother and sisters' selfishness.*

Mr Fitzwilliam Darcy [p. 47]

1

His background and manner	1: *Mr Darcy is the wealthy and good-looking son of an upper-class family.* 2: *He gives an impression of arrogance.*
His behaviour and what he thinks or says about others	1: *He is often reserved and silent, liable to give himself away through body language rather than in speech.* 2: *He prefers his own circle to people he doesn't know.*
His relationships	1: *He is a good brother, good friend, good employer.* 2: *He uses good manners to keep people at a distance.* 3: *He falls in love with Elizabeth.*

3

Evidence	Quotation
a) *Blushing is usually considered to be a sign of physical attraction.*	*'Their eyes instantly met and the cheeks of each were overspread with the deepest blush.'*
b) *Darcy asks after the Bennet family.*	*'To speak with such civility, to enquire after her family!'*
c) *Darcy asks to be introduced to the Gardiners.*	*'He asked her, if she would do him the honour of introducing him to her friends'*
d) *Darcy asks to be allowed to introduce his sister to Elizabeth.*	*'Will you allow me, or do I ask too much, to introduce my sister to your acquaintance?'*

Jane Bennet [p. 48]

1&2 beautiful (Vol. 1, Ch. 2, p. 8), modest (Vol. 1, Ch. 4, p. 10), kindly (p. 10), even-tempered (Vol. 1, Ch. 6, p. 15), reserved (Vol. 1, Ch. 6, p. 16), trusting (Vol. 1, Ch. 21, p. 100), calm (Vol. 1, Ch. 23, p. 109), sensitive (Vol. 2, Ch. 1, p. 112), discreet (Vol. 2, Ch. 16, p. 181), caring (Vol. 3, Ch. 5, p. 235), loving (Vol. 3, Ch. 13, p. 286)

3 *Jane Bennet's* **friendship** *with Caroline Bingley gives the reader some insight into her* **character***. Jane is a naturally* **trusting** *person and always thinks* **well** *of other people where she can. She doesn't see that Caroline is jealous and snobbish and assumes she is* **sincere** *when she drops hints that her brother prefers Miss Darcy. Jane however believes strongly in the importance of good* **manners,** *so when Caroline fails to respond to her letters and calls in London and then is deliberately rude, Jane begins to see her as she is. She is honest in admitting to Elizabeth that she has been* **mistaken***.*

Mr Charles Bingley [p. 49]

1

Quality	Moment in novel	Quotation
a) Friendly	*The assembly at Meryton*	*'Mr Bingley had soon made himself acquainted with all the principal people in the room.'*
b) Easy-going	*Discussion at Netherfield*	*'When I am in the country [...] I never wish to leave it; and when I am in town it is pretty much the same.'*
c) Modest	*Darcy's letter*	*'Bingley has great natural modesty, with a stronger dependence on my judgement than his own.'*
d) Loving	*After his proposal to Jane*	*'[Elizabeth] had to listen to all he had to say, of his own happiness, and Jane's perfections'*

2 *When Mr Bennet describes Jane and Bingley as being so* **'complying'** *and* **'generous'** *that they are likely to be cheated by their servants and to get into debt, Jane is shocked yet the reader will know that Mr Bennet's teasing remarks have a kernel of truth. We have already seen Bingley's tendency towards* **hastiness** *when leaving Netherfield for London and his* **persuadability** *or even (in Elizabeth's opinion)* **weakness** *in yielding to his sisters' and Darcy's advice not to return. The narrator has told us of his* **impulsive** *approach to buying or renting property and his* **casual** *reliance on his housekeeper to make all the practical arrangements. He is obviously* **generous** *as he provides a home for both his sisters and agrees* **unhesitatingly** *to Lydia's request for a ball.*

Mr and Mrs Bennet [p. 50]

1 a) F; b) T; c) T; d) NEE; e) T; f) F; g) NEE

2

His and her general personality (using either your own or the narrator's words)	1: *Mr Bennet is unpredictable, witty, intelligent, self-contained.* 2: *Mrs Bennet is shallow, scheming, bad-tempered, hypochondriac.*
His and her behaviour in public	1: *He humiliates Mary in public.* 2: *She talks loudly about her hopes for Jane's marriage to Bingley and is rude about Darcy.*
Their relationship either day to day or in times of stress	1: *He teases her and sets traps for her to fall into. She doesn't understand him.* 2: *In times of stress he goes to his library; she stays in her room.*

Mr William Collins [p. 51]

1

Quality	Moment in novel	Quotation
a) Pomposity	Talking to Mr Bennet about his flattery of Lady Catherine	'I am happy on every occasion to offer these little delicate compliments which are always acceptable to ladies.' (Vol. 1, Ch. 14, p. 55)
b) Apparent humility	Narrator analyses him when he has arrived at Longbourn	His early subjection by his father 'had given him originally great humility of manner' (Vol. 1, Ch. 15, p. 57)
c) Actual conceit	After Elizabeth has refused him	'He thought too well of himself to comprehend on what motive his cousin could refuse him' (Vol. 1, Ch. 20, p. 94)
d) Unforgiving	Reaction to Lydia's elopement	Advises Mr Bennet to 'throw off your unworthy child from your affection for ever' (Vol. 3, Ch. 6, p. 244)

2 'My situation in life, my connections': *self-centred* – shown by the repetition of the word 'my'

'other than highly desirable', 'highly in my favour': *conceited* – shown by repetition of 'highly' and also the opening phrase 'it does not appear to me'

'My situation in life ... highly in my favour: *materialistic* – shown by his list of 'circumstances' – his 'situation ... connections ... relationship'); he never mentions love.

'in spite of your manifold attractions': *ponderous and materialistic* – his choice of words 'manifold attractions' suggests that he sees Elizabeth's beauty and intelligence as properties which she may be offering him as part of a bargain.

Mr George Wickham [p. 52]

1 charming (Vol. 1, Ch. 15, p. 59), good-looking (p. 59), friendly (p.59), polite (p. 59), gentlemanlike (Vol. 1, Ch. 16, p. 62), indiscreet (Vol. 1, Ch. 16, p. 64), mercenary (Vol. 2, Ch. 4, p. 128), extravagant (Vol. 2, Ch. 12, p. 166), vicious (p.166), idle (Vol. 2, Ch. 12, p. 167), unscrupulous (p. 167), vengeful (Vol. 2, Ch. 12, p. 168)

3

Wickham's quality of shamelessness is never more apparent than when he and Lydia visit **Longbourn** after their marriage. Jane, Elizabeth and Mr Bennet had all expected him to appear **embarrassed** or even apologetic. Instead the couple arrive full of 'easy assurance' and expect to be as welcome as if nothing **shocking** had occurred. When Wickham is alone with **Elizabeth** he tries once again to gain her sympathy for his misfortunes in the past and repeats his allegations of cruel treatment by **Mr Darcy**. Once he realises that she knows the truth he pretends to be gallant and **affectionate** but never mentions the subject again. Mr Bennet describes him ironically as a 'fine fellow' who 'simpers, and **smirks**, and makes love to us all'. (Vol. 3, Ch. 11, p. 272)

Charlotte Lucas [p. 53]

1

Her background, age and manner	1: Charlotte is the eldest daughter of Sir William and Lady Lucas.
	2: She is twenty-seven years old, plain, sensible and intelligent.
Her opinions and behaviour	1: She has clear opinions and is ready to tease and debate with Elizabeth.
	2: She is tactful when she realises the awkward situation caused by Elizabeth's refusal of Mr Collins. She also sees how to profit from it.
Her relationships	1: She values her friendship with Elizabeth but her own interests come first.
	2: She has to use all her tact and strategic skills to cope when living with Mr Collins.

Lydia Bennet [p. 53]

1

Quality	Moment in the novel	Quotation
Overconfident	On first appearance	'Oh,' said Lydia stoutly, 'I am not afraid' (Vol. 1, Ch. 2, p. 5)
Lively	When playing cards at Mrs Philips's house	'She soon grew too [...] eager in making bets' (Vol. 1, Ch. 16, p. 63).
Attention-seeking	When travelling to Longbourn after her marriage	'I [...] took off my glove [...] so he might see the ring, and then I bowed and smiled like any thing.' (Vol. 3, Ch. 9, p. 260)
Insensitive	When visiting Longbourn after her marriage	(to Jane) 'you must go lower, because I am a married woman' (Vol. 3, Ch. 9, p. 260)

Caroline Bingley and Louisa Hurst [p. 54]

1 a) *Elizabeth's first impression of both Caroline Bingley and her sister Louisa is that they are supercilious towards others.* (Vol. 1, Ch. 6, p. 15)

b) *Caroline and Louisa can be agreeable when they choose but are described by the narrator as 'proud and conceited'.* (Vol. 1, Ch. 4, p. 11)

c) *Caroline and Louisa prefer to forget that their fortunes were earned in trade.* (Vol. 1, Ch. 4, p. 11)

d) *Caroline tries to ingratiate herself with Mr Darcy by criticising other people and agreeing with everything he says.* (Vol. 1, Ch. 8, p. 31)

e) *Caroline's jealous criticisms of Elizabeth to Mr Darcy finally result in hurt to herself.* (Vol. 3, Ch. 3 , p. 223)

Lady Catherine de Bourgh [p. 54]

Mr Collins: generous (Vol. 1, Ch. 13, p. 51), affable (Vol. 1, Ch. 13, p. 54), charming (Vol. 2, Ch. 5, p. 131), music-loving (Vol. 2, Ch. 8, p. 143).

ANSWERS

Others: proud (Vol. 1, Ch. 14, p. 54), gracious (p. 54), arrogant (Vol. 1, Ch. 16, p. 69), conceited (p. 69), dictatorial (p. 69), insolent (p. 69), authoritative (Vol. 2, Ch. 6, p. 135), impertinent (Vol. 2, Ch. 6, p. 136), self-centred (Vol. 2, Ch. 6, p. 138), musically ignorant (Vol. 2, Ch. 8, p. 144), interfering (Vol. 2, Ch. 7, p. 140), insulting (Vol. 3, Ch. 14, p. 296).

Mr Collins and others: condescending (Vol. 1, Ch. 14, p. 54), stately (Vol. 2, Ch. 6, p. 135), frank (Vol. 3, Ch. 14, p. 292).

PART FOUR: THEMES, CONTEXTS AND SETTINGS [pp. 56–63]

Themes [pp. 56–8]

1 *Jane Austen offers the reader many **variations** on the theme of pride. The people at the Meryton Assembly judge **Mr Darcy** to be proud because he is reluctant to **dance** or join in conversation. When the Bennets and the Lucases are discussing him the following day Charlotte Lucas says Darcy has a **right** to be proud because of his good family and good income. She is presenting pride as something closer to **self-esteem**. Arrogance, as exemplified by **Lady Catherine**, is presented as a fault and Darcy admits he has needed Elizabeth to cure him of it. Mr Collins, who appears so humble, is far too **conceited** to believe that Elizabeth does not find his proposal attractive, whereas rich Mr Bingley's quality of **modesty** is so extreme that he trusts Darcy's opinion of Jane and not his own feelings for her.*

2 a) marriage; b) manners; c) prejudice; d) pride

3 a) *Elizabeth's comment to Charlotte is linked to the theme of marriage because they have been discussing Jane and Bingley's growing attraction. Charlotte believes that Jane should pretend more than she feels in order to 'fix him'. She discounts love and asserts instead that happiness in marriage is merely a matter of chance. Austen's effect is ironic as Charlotte does in fact 'act that way herself'.*

b) *Lady Catherine's remark is linked to the theme of manners because she is critical of the way that Elizabeth, her social inferior, addresses her so confidently.*

Austen's effect is ironic, as Lady Catherine gives her own opinion rudely throughout the novel.

4 a) *Darcy accuses various members of the Bennet family of a 'total want of propriety'. By 'propriety' he means behaving politely in public, avoiding personal comments or drawing attention to oneself. (Vol. 2, Ch. 12, p. 164)*

b) *Good manners are linked to self-control and sensitivity to other people's feelings. Mrs Bennet lacks all of these. This means that she is rude in public (to Darcy) and hurtful in private (to Jane).*

c) *When Elizabeth's eyes are opened to Wickham's true character she uses the words 'impropriety' and 'indelicacy' because she realises that she and Mr Wickham transgressed the conventions of politeness in their first conversation about Mr Darcy. (Vol. 2, Ch. 13, p. 171)*

5 a) *Elizabeth is prejudiced because she is judging by appearance and has been misled by her negative first impression of Darcy and positive one of Wickham. In the dialogue Austen makes the most of the contrast between Jane's carefulness and Elizabeth's tendency to be hasty and overconfident.*

b) *The opening sentence of the novel introduces the linked themes of marriage and money. Austen's sequence of clauses is significant. 'In possession of a good fortune' comes before 'must be in want of a wife', suggesting that a wife is another type of possession. The words 'truth' and 'universally acknowledged' assert that these rules are known and understood by everyone but the emphasis may also*

include an element of irony, as if the author is distancing herself from this materialistic attitude.

6 a) Elizabeth is speaking strongly about Lydia as she hopes to encourage her father to take seriously his responsibilities as the head of their family. She and the reader know that this tarnishing of the family reputation has already happened and both Jane and Elizabeth's chances have been affected by it. Elizabeth however asserts that she is not speaking personally but generally.

b) On one level Mr Collins is correct – family disgrace affects all its members. He does not add a question mark to Lady Catherine's reported comment because both he and she consider it a statement of fact. The irony is that, if it were a question, the answer would be Mr Darcy, Lady Catherine's own nephew.

Contexts [pp. 59–60]

1 a) 1813; b) Regency; c) gentry; d) clergyman; e) dependent

2 a) The presence of the Militia in Meryton is the only evidence, in the novel, that England is a country at war with France.

b) Reading was essential to give Austen both entertainment and a wide view of the world beyond her own village. In the novel a character's attitude to books often sheds light on their personality.

c) Being a woman certainly made it more difficult for Austen to achieve publication and she needed the help of her father and brothers. It is also likely to have made it harder for her to find the time and space in which to write. 'Work' for a woman of Austen's class meant needlework and she generally had no room of her own, not even her own bedroom.

3

Point /detail	Evidence	Effect or explanation
1: Elizabeth is surprised by Mrs Reynolds's friendliness.	'a respectable-looking elderly woman, much less fine and more civil than she had any notion of finding her'	Mrs Reynolds's approachability is reassuring after the grandeur of the house and the park. This prepares the reader to see Pemberley as a family home.
2: Mrs Reynolds provides a first-hand account of Darcy as a child.	'I have never had a cross word from him in my life, and I have known him since he was four years old'.	We may be as surprised by this statement as Elizabeth and may therefore begin to rethink our own understanding of Mr Darcy.
3: Austen suggests that the housekeeper's opinions are solidly based and credible.	'What praise is more valuable than the praise of an intelligent servant?'	Mentioning Mrs Reynolds's class highlights the fact she has a different perspective but it is one to be trusted.

Settings [pp. 61–2]

Pemberley: Home of the Darcy family and their household. Also of Mr Wickham in his youth. By the end of the novel Pemberley has become Elizabeth's own family home. Volume: 3.

Rosings: Home of Lady Catherine de Bourgh and her daughter. Volume: 2.

Hunsford Parsonage: Home of Mr and Mrs Collins (formerly Charlotte Lucas). Volume: 2.

Longbourn: Home of the Bennet family. Volume: 1, especially, but also important in Volumes 2 and 3.

Meryton: Nearby village and home of Mr and Mrs Philips, Mrs Bennet's relations. Volume: 1.

Netherfield Park: Home of Mr Bingley. Volume: 1.

2 a) Charlotte has already been presented as a domesticated person (helping with the mince pies) and in Volume 2 she is shown enjoying managing her own house and her parish duties. She is also clever at managing her daily life to keep her husband out of her way as much as possible.

b) Rosings is described as being situated 'on rising ground' (Vol. 2, Ch. 5, p. 130) and seems to have been designed to impress. Austen's presentation of Rosings gives the impression that it is a place where things matter more than people and what they cost is as important as what they are.

c) Privacy is harder for women characters to achieve than for men as they do not have a study or a library to retreat to and most unmarried women would be expected to share a bedroom. Elizabeth often gets away from other people by walking, but Austen shows Jane Bennet, in particular, as oppressed by the constant demands of her mother.

3

Point /detail	Evidence	Effect /explanation
1: The setting combines natural beauty with discreet human management.	'She had never seen a place for which nature had done more, or where natural beauty had been so little counteracted by an awkward taste.'	We view Pemberley for the first time through Elizabeth's eyes. As well as revealing her personal feelings, this shows her appreciation for the Romantic movement in landscape.
2: The furnishing is favourably compared to Rosings. Things have been chosen for beauty and use.	'it was neither gaudy nor uselessly fine; with less of splendour, and more real elegance than the furniture of Rosings'	Again we are looking through Elizabeth's eyes. For her, good taste is more important than money and she sees this as a place where she could be happy.
3: A big estate needs good management. Lady Catherine 'scolded' her tenants: Mr Darcy is kinder to his.	Mrs Reynolds: 'He is the best landlord, and the best master'.	Mr Darcy is as 'affable' to the poor – as his father was before him. There is plenty of evidence that he follows his father's example, even retaining Wickham's portrait.

PART FIVE: FORM, STRUCTURE AND LANGUAGE [pp. 64–9]

Form [p. 64]

1 a) a novel; b) borrowed from circulating libraries; c) epistolary novels; d) essays

2 a) *Pride and Prejudice* can be described as a romantic novel because it focuses on the relationship between a hero and heroine and it has a happy ending. As in many romantic novels, the hero and heroine have to overcome a series of difficulties before they can be together.

b) *Pride and Prejudice* is realistic about the lack of opportunities for women outside marriage. Charlotte Lucas is shown taking a materialistic view of marriage as the only respectable way of gaining a home of her own and avoiding being dependent on her male relatives. The novel is also realistic about the harsh social consequences (for women) of living with a man without marriage: for example, the gossips of Meryton expected Lydia to 'come upon the town' (i.e. become a prostitute).

c) *Pride and Prejudice* has many comic characters such as Mr Collins, Lady Catherine, Sir William Lucas, Mrs Bennet, Caroline Bingley. The attitude of the narrator is ironic, which means that people are viewed in such a way that their 'follies and nonsense, whims and inconsistencies' (Vol. 1, Ch. 11, p. 46) become obvious. However, the fact that other characters such as Charlotte Lucas have no choice other than to live with these caricature characters makes the comedy much darker.

Structure [p. 65]

1

Scene	Location	Volume number
1: Elizabeth enjoys lively conversation and possible mutual attraction with George Wickham.	Meryton and Longbourn	1
2: Elizabeth and Charlotte discuss their different views of marriage.	Longbourn	1
3: Mr Bennet warns Elizabeth against marriage without respecting her 'partner in life'.	Longbourn	3
4: Elizabeth begs her father not to allow Lydia to go to Brighton.	Longbourn	2
5: Mr Darcy finally loses patience with Caroline Bingley.	Pemberley	3

2 a) Letters and their reception are crucial in advancing the action. Caroline Bingley's letter announcing her and her brother's departure from Netherfield arrives unexpectedly and as well as learning about the changed situation, the reader sees the distress this news causes Jane. Darcy's letter to Elizabeth and Jane's two letters announcing Lydia's elopement are other major developments in the story which are seen in the context of the recipient's emotions.

b) Bingley and Darcy appear together, with Bingley appearing amiable and Darcy arrogant. Mr Collins and Mr Wickham are also introduced one after another, with Wickham appearing the much more attractive character. In both these cases first impressions are not always accurate – and this is part of the theme of pride and prejudice.

c) Austen uses coincidence and a network of relationships to link the strands of her plot. Lady Catherine is Mr Collins's patron and also Darcy's aunt. Mr Wickham's father was Darcy's father's steward. Elizabeth's aunt spent her childhood in Derbyshire, and Elizabeth accompanies the Gardiners on holiday there. All these factors bring hero and heroine together in different locations to learn more about each other.

Language [pp. 66–8]

1 a) 'Michaelmas' – 29 September, an annual quarter day for business transactions; b) 'entail' – legal restriction on who can

ANSWERS

inherit a family's property; c) 'in his regimentals' – in his uniform; d) 'mortification' – humiliation; e) 'propriety' – proper social conduct; f) 'affable' – approachable; g) 'come upon the town' – become a prostitute

3&4

Feeling	Moment in the novel	Quotation
1: Bliss	When Elizabeth and Darcy finally admit that they love each other and want to marry	'They walked on, _without knowing_ in what direction. There was _too much to be thought, and felt_' (Vol. 3, Ch. 16, p. 303)
2: Outrage	When Elizabeth rejects Mr Darcy	'And _this_,' cried Darcy, as he walked with _quick steps_ across the room, 'is your opinion of _me_!' (Vol. 2, Ch. 11, p. 159)
3: Shock	When Wickham first tells his story	'_Good heavens_!' cried Elizabeth, 'but _how_ could that be?' (Vol. 1, Ch. 16, p. 65)

5 a) Mrs Bennet; b) Caroline Bingley; c) Lydia Bennet; d) Lady Catherine de Bourgh; e) Mr Collins; f) Mr Bennet; g) Charlotte Lucas

6

Example or quotation	Literary technique	Meaning/effect
1: 'One has got all the goodness, and the other all the appearance of it' (Vol. 2, Ch. 17, p. 186)	Balanced sentence	Here 'all the goodness' is answered by 'all the appearance'. This shows the speaker's intelligence.
2: 'You refuse to obey the claims of duty, honour, and gratitude.' (Vol. 3, Ch. 15, p. 296)	Rhetorical pattern of three	Lady Catherine is shown using the power of a pattern of three nouns to try to bully Elizabeth.
3: 'Lady Lucas was enquiring [...] after the welfare and poultry of her eldest daughter' (Vol. 2, Ch. 16, p. 183)	Use of concrete nouns	Lady Lucas's small mindedness is suggested by her equal interest in Charlotte's chickens as well as her happiness.

7

Technique	Example	Effect
1: Use of abstract nouns	'she was not able to gratify him with any sign of repentance'	The word 'repentance' is a strong word with a religious overtone which gives an ironic effect as it is so far from what she feels.
2: Use of concrete nouns	'He could number the fields in every direction, and could tell how many trees were in every distant clump.'	The reader is with Elizabeth as she listens to Mr Collins pointing out these ordinary things in such an overly detailed way. We share Elizabeth's perception of Mr Collins's small mind.

| 3: Use of unspoken communication | 'She involuntarily turned her eye on Charlotte.' | Austen indicates the things that the friends can no longer talk about through Elizabeth's 'involuntary' glance and Charlotte's occasional 'faint blush'. |

PART SIX: PROGRESS BOOSTER [pp. 70–83]

Expressing and explaining ideas [pp. 70–1]

2 Student A: Level – high (H). This is well expressed and makes it clear that the student has grasped the author's techniques and intentions. The quotation is appropriate and fluently embedded.

Student B: Level – lower (L). This student has understood some elements of Lydia's character but has entirely missed the author's disapproval. The quotation is not therefore appropriately used or embedded.

3 The word 'gentleman-like' convinces the reader that Darcy has indeed listened to what Elizabeth said and agrees with her that this is a quality which he lacked when he made his first, arrogant proposal.

6 Elizabeth **is aware** that her parents' marriage is neither satisfying nor admirable. The narrator **tells us** that they married because Mr Bennet was attracted by Mrs Bennet's 'appearance of good humour' as well as by her good looks. She **explains** that when he discovered how shallow and ignorant his wife was he took refuge in his books and in secretly laughing at her. Austen **comments** 'this is not the sort of happiness which a man would in general wish to owe to his wife'.

Making inferences and interpretations [p. 72]

1 Jane Bennet is presented as a character who is almost too good to be true but yet she remains human and sympathetic. At the end of Volume One she is suffering both from Bingley's desertion and from her mother's constant allusions to his absence. 'Oh! that my dear mother had more command of herself,' she says after what the narrator describes as a 'longer than usual irritation'. The very fact that Jane bursts out in this way suggests how sensitive she is, and the depth of her pain.

2 b) is thinking of Mr Darcy at this moment because she is more attracted to him than she realises and he is there, unconsciously, in her mind.

Writing about context [p. 73]

1 b) Because it makes the link between Caroline Bingley's social situation and her character.

2 c) that Mr Collins is 'neither sensible nor agreeable [...] but still he [will] be her husband'.

Structure and linking of paragraphs [pp. 74–5]

1 Even before Mr Collins arrives, Austen makes it clear that he is both ignorant and conceited. 'Can he be a sensible man, sir?' Elizabeth asks her father as soon as she has listened to Mr Collins's letter. Her word 'sensible' means rational but also self-aware or sensitive. Mr Collins is none of those things.

2 Jane Austen presents Mr Bingley as an 'amiable' young man. Her frequent use of this word sums up Bingley's qualities of friendliness, generosity and a wish to see the best in everyone. His behaviour at the Meryton assembly shows his capacity for enjoyment and this willingness to be pleased. *The slight exaggeration of his reported response that he 'had never met with pleasanter people or prettier girls in his life' may alert the reader to the fact that Bingley may be volatile, lacking in judgement or even weak.*

3 *Although Kitty Bennet is not one of the novel's main characters, Austen presents her as someone who is influenced by other people and by her environment and who may therefore be capable of change. Kitty is regularly described as 'fretful'. This suggests that she is not happy with her life. It's a measure of Mr and Mrs Bennet's failure as parents that it is Jane and Elizabeth who finally enable Kitty to develop when they have better homes than Longbourn in which to nurture her.*

Writing skills [pp. 76–7]

3 *Austen has already **depicted** Lady Catherine as a character who is used to having her own way. Only Elizabeth's quickness with **dialogue** enables her to cope with Lady Catherine's verbal bullying when she calls at **Longbourn**. Finally however, after the **rhetorical** question, 'Are the shades of **Pemberley** to be **thus** polluted?' Elizabeth resorts to **negativity** and silence – thus demonstrating her **capacity** for self-restraint.*

4 *Meryton is the place where people go to have fun, such as attending an assembly or going shopping or visiting **Aunt Philips** for*

a gossip. **The** country life is so mundane for the girls **that** it **isn't** surprising **they're** glad when the regiment arrives. **After** they've left for **Brighton** it's a month before **Kitty** 'can enter **Meryton** without tears', notices **Elizabeth**.

5 Student B

6 *It **is** fortunate that Mrs Bennet and Lydia **are unaware** that Elizabeth **is pleading** with Mr Bennet to forbid Lydia to go to Brighton. Elizabeth **is afraid** that Lydia **will become** 'the most determined flirt' whilst Lydia **is already dreaming** of 'tenderly flirting with at least six officers at once'.*

Tackling exam tasks [p. 78]

1 Question: *How* does *Austen* present the *links between social class, money and manners*?

Write about:

● The *different social position, wealth* and *behaviour of characters*
● The *methods* Austen uses to *highlight* these *links*

Sample answers [pp. 80–1]

1 Student A: Expert viewpoint 1; Student B: Expert viewpoint 2

3 Student A: Expert viewpoint 2; Student B: Expert viewpoint 1